Praise for The Circle of Seven

This slim novella carries a hefty wallop. Drawing on decades as a parish pastor, author Ennis invites his readers into the heart-wrenching world of contemporary ministry. It is a pain-filled world which demands superhuman responses from fragile, breakable humans. He asks the penetrating question: Who ministers to ministers in their times of anguish? His answer is to look to the presence of the divine in the midst of a circle of fragile, broken, and re-formed peers.

— Donald A. Luidens, PhD
Senior Research Fellow, Van Raalte Institute
Professor of Sociology, Emeritus, Hope College

This book is a moving, raw, authentic primer on the realities of pastoral care in both church and society, and the critical need for clergy to guard against isolation, guilt, and shame. Rev. Ennis brings to vibrant, emotive life the redemptive power of sharing our stories with supportive, like-minded colleagues and the ongoing healing work that results. Beyond the case studies, *Circle of Seven* offers a model for creating sacred, vulnerable space together that will spark the imagination of emerging and established ministry leaders alike who are seeking to build circles of trust and healing in their own unique contexts.

— Rev. Elizabeth Testa
Women's Transformation and Leadership
Reformed Church in America

Circle of Seven is an engaging and moving story. While a work of fiction, it clearly draws on Mark Ennis's lifetime of pastoral care for parishioners, counselees, and colleagues; he clearly understands the feelings of people in crisis. This book could be used as a textbook for pastors and those training for ministry in how to care for one another and the true meaning of "covenant community." It could also be a primer for those not in ministry, giving them a glimpse of the pain and humanity with which people in ministry—in any faith tradition—grapple each and every day.

— **James Hart Brumm**
General Editor,
The Historical Series of the
Reformed Church in America

Reading *The Circle of Seven* will take you on a journey toward your own healing. The author skillfully draws the reader[s] to reflect on our own need[s] for support and affirmation. This book is must reading, especially for caregivers.

— **Reverend Willard Walden Christopher Ashley, Sr.,**
MDiv., DMin., SCP
Vice President for Strategic Institutional Initiatives
Associate Professor of Practical Theology
New Brunswick Theological Seminary

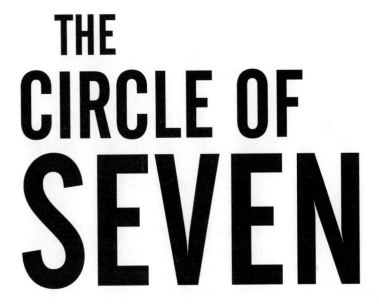

THE
CIRCLE OF
SEVEN

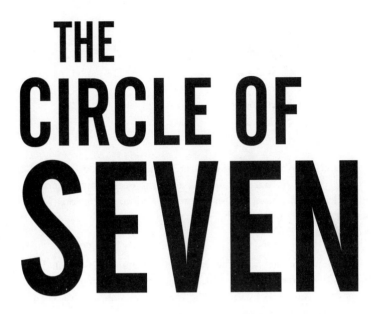

THE CIRCLE OF SEVEN

WHEN HIS

SERVANTS

ARE WEAK

By

REV. MARK
WILLIAM ENNIS

Deep River
B O O K S

Published by Deep River Books
Sisters, Oregon
www.deepriverbooks.com

ISBN – 13: 9781632694829
LOC: 2018955201

Cover Design by Jason Enterline

Printed in the USA
2018—First Edition
27 26 25 24 23 22 21 20 19 18   10 9 8 7 6 5 4 3 2 1

Dedication

This book is dedicated to ministers who do the hard work of pastoral care. Unlike the more visible aspects of ministry, this work is often invisible. It is difficult work, and those who do it must depend not on their own strength but on their relationship with Jesus, as well as with trusted Christian colleagues. This is a tribute to those Christian men and women.

My Thanks

I thank my family, who put up with my long hours writing this book and my moods as I remembered some difficult times.

My thanks also to Nancy and John, my writing partners, who helped me edit this work.

Table of Contents

1: Will He Kill Himself?. 13

2: I Hurt a Child 19

3: Assembling a Circle 29

4: The Depressed and the Hippie 43

5: Assembled Circle 49

6: She Was Beaten by My Pride 55

7: Baby Killer. 65

8: A Non-Mother's Pain 75

9: Silent Supper 87

10: Evicted Children 91

11: Abducted 101

12: Millstones for the Neck 113

13: Christ's Healing 123

14: Welcome Home 133

1

Will He Kill Himself?

The intercom buzzed, interrupting my thoughts and my typing. I didn't want to be disturbed this morning as I prepared my annual report, and I clenched my jaw; I had left instructions with Helen to make sure that I wasn't disturbed.

It buzzed a second time, and I let out a sigh. Helen could be persistent when she wanted to be. I swiveled my leather chair to face the oak desk before pressing the button.

"What is it, Helen?"

"William de Plore is on the phone for you."

"Can't you have him call back?"

"He sounds like he needs you," she said.

I trusted her instinct. Besides efficiency, Helen had the gift of discernment. I had learned that six years ago when we first began to work together. Gray-haired and distinguished, she was more than a secretary—she was a mother, a big sister, a confidant, and sometimes a spiritual advisor. Helen could hear the soul behind the voice and see the spirit behind the eyes.

"Is he OK?"

"I don't think so. Please talk to him."

"OK."

The light of my telephone flashed.

"Hello, Will. How are you?"

"I need to talk to you. What time works for you?"

He sounded sad, depressed, and spiritually dead. It was unlike the upbeat, rowdy self that he usually presented. William was a ten-year veteran of ministry and a product of the city of Newark. He had a street side to him, but also a kind and gentle spirit. I had never heard his voice sound so lifeless.

"Are you OK? Are you in trouble?"

"I'm not in trouble, Jack, but I'm really down. I need to talk to you."

"Where are you? Are you close by?"

"I'm at the church office."

Quickly I estimated the distance to his church in my head. If I remembered correctly, the church was more than an hour away.

"How soon can you be here and still drive safely?"

"Probably an hour and a quarter."

"I'll make the time free. "

"Thank you, Jack."

"You're welcome." I paused before continuing, "Will, I need to ask you something straightforward and I need an honest answer. You sound depressed. Are you going to hurt yourself?"

He hesitated for a moment, then told me he wasn't planning to. Pausing for him was uncharacteristic. William never slowed down when speaking. If anything, I had sometimes wished that he would stop before blurting things out, but it was against his urban nature and upbringing.

"Bring in some donuts and I'll have the coffee pot on," I instructed, giving him a task to keep him connected. I didn't like how he sounded, and knew that I might be walking in the valley of the shadow of death that King David had written about.

"Thanks," he said. "I'll see you then."

He hung up and I put the phone down. My body was tense; I knew that I couldn't go back to my report. Pastoral care of my ministers took priority in my life. It was the reason that I took the job of Synod Executive, a combination of administrator and bishop ministering to pastors. It was one of the loves of my life. It just never got any easier.

I was ordained in the 1970s, when America was still trying to be a Christian country. I'm not sure that it ever was, but at least it pretended to be. Churches and ministers were respected and validated. This has changed over the years, and it has taken a toll on the ministers I care for. Overwork, limited validation, declining congregations, and a pagan/secular culture all have drained many ministers spiritually. I try to help my ministers bond and hold one another up, as the early disciples did when they gathered together for mutual support. Sometimes I succeed. Sometimes I fail.

Will was now serving his second charge. The first was a small, rural church in New York state. Now he had returned to his home state of New Jersey and was dealing with a small, impoverished, urban congregation in North Jersey within my synod. I liked him and appreciated his spirit and zeal. I also knew that he felt too much and could be hurt. I was afraid that this sensitivity was hurting him now.

"I'm going for a walk, Helen. I'll be back."

Helen did not react with any surprise. Every secretary that I had ever had got used to my habit of walking outside or pacing inside. "OK, Jack, I'll take messages."

I left the safety of the synod office, housed in an old church, and began my walk. I think more clearly when I am in motion, especially when I am walking. Perhaps it comes from my training as a youth on the family farm in Iowa; we were in motion all day long. I needed a walk to clear my head, and to prepare for Will. I filled my largest and favorite coffee mug, the one with the picture of my theological hero John Calvin, and left my office.

I knew where I was going: in circles. Usually my walks were circles around the blocks surrounding my churches. I was far enough away to think, but close enough if I was needed.

What could Will need? In my early days of ministry, the worst thing that ever happened to clergy was marital troubles. The lives of pastoral families were never easy. Pastors were on call every hour of every day. Wives—and now with women's ordination, husbands—were subjected to the expectations of the parish as well, even though they had no compensation. Such pressures often wreaked havoc. Even children of the parsonage were not exempt from the stress of being the "minister's kid."

Times had changed and clergy issues have gotten more serious. Infidelity was no longer unknown—or at least we talk about it more. Old-timers tell me that secrets were kept in past generations. Now we don't keep any secrets. During the past decade the Roman Catholic scandals have made all of us in churches a bit paranoid and under suspicion. People unrelated to faith groups can't tell the difference between the Roman Catholic Church and other churches. I hoped and prayed that we did not have a scandal coming.

Definitions of misconduct had changed over the years, and that only complicated matters for clergy. In the 1950s, single white men attended seminary, graduated, and began serving a church. Frequently they found their wives from among the young ladies of the congregation. With churches and ministers being so honored in those days, women swooned over these new members of the cloth, each hoping to be residing in the parsonage. It was a good system to ensure that ministers would not have to be single and that new babies would come for the Sunday school.

Of course, the system had flaws as well. Great fights could break out among the women vying to marry the pastor. Pastoral conflicts could be devastating for a wife who had grown up in the congregation. New understandings of power abuse and "chains of command" caused alterations to this system. Now ministers were no longer allowed to date people within the congregation, for fear of abusing their power. I understand the reasoning behind this but am afraid this will lead to either marriages outside of the faith, which will cause parsonage difficulties, or many more unmarried ministers. I hope that we don't wind up with single, sexually frustrated clergy, as the Roman Catholic Church has had in recent years. That would lead to many victims and all kinds of headaches.

I walked around the block and sipped my coffee as I thought, worried, prayed, and sang. One block away was a small playground. A mother watched her child play in a sandbox. I felt sad as the mother saw me walking, and reflexively moved closer to her daughter. Our culture now assumes that men in clergy shirts must be predators. I smiled and nodded to the woman. And kept on my way.

Maybe it was the difference between the midwest where I grew up and the east where I now lived. Maybe it was the difference of the decades that had passed. Maybe it was the difference between a largely Protestant area and the Catholic area in which I now resided. Whatever the reason, every member of the clergy used to be greeted like royalty from children and parents. Now they are people to be avoided. No wonder our clergy had such esteem issues.

I continued my walk for an hour, returned to my office, and prayerfully waited for Will— and the adventure God would take us on.

2
I Hurt a Child

The intercom buzzed and Helen's voice intoned, "Will is here to see you."

"Thank you, Helen," I said to the box on my desk as I looked at my clock—Will was twenty minutes early. Yes, people in dire circumstances would be anxious to see me, but he was also compulsively early. I knew that from past meetings.

I rose, crossed the length of my office, and opened the door. Over Helen's desk I could see him sitting in the plastic chair, looking disheveled, and holding a box of donuts. His eyes were narrowed and he looked sad.

"Come on in, Will."

Will was one of the ministers who lightened up meetings with his humor and his rowdy personality. Now he looked like a dead man walking. It hurt my heart to see him in pain.

"Sit down. I'll fetch the coffee."

He flopped in the leather chair in front of the coffee table and sighed. I picked up the coffee pot, filled mine and poured him a cup in one of our logo mugs. I set the two mugs on the coffee table, turned back to the sideboard, grabbed a stack of napkins, and set them on the table. Only then did I sit myself on the chair across from Will.

"Thank you for the donuts." I opened the box and saw that six of the dozen were French crullers. They were a gift for me. It is no secret that these were the only donuts that I truly enjoyed. "Crullers!" I exclaimed. "Thank you."

He smiled a bit slightly and mumbled a "you're welcome." How unlike his normal self he was this morning. I waited for him to begin as I sipped coffee and ate a cruller. It was a "therapeutic silence." Religious people call it the "holy moment." I secretly call it the "moment of agony." I hate these silences. It was an issue for me when I took chaplaincy-training courses. I feel anxiety during silence. I grew up in a loud and rowdy home. Silence only was heard when there was anger, when family members stopped talking to one another. I have grown to accept silence but never to like it. For me it feels like a horrible waste of time. I stared at the clock, waited three minutes and I could not wait any longer.

"Will, I appreciate the crullers and I hope you like the coffee, but if you have something on your mind you might want to start talking. I'm not a Vulcan and can't read your mind."

He smiled slightly and looked up at me before shifting anxiously in his chair. "It's hard to talk about."

"I'm sure it is, but why don't you try?"

He clutched the coffee mug, staring at his shoes, and after taking three deep cleansing breaths, never once being able to look at me, he began to talk.

"Jack, I hurt a child," he told me, and my heart dropped. My mind paused; I hoped that I had not heard him correctly. It was my worst nightmare. Visions of molested children, police intervention, and court cases all sprang up into my head. I envisioned his wife and his children devastated. I could see myself in front of television cameras, and reporters asking me questions as Will was hauled off to jail.

I started to speak but halted as he leaned forward and began to speak again. "I feel horrible," he said, tears forming in his eyes. He paused as he placed his mug next to him and put his hands over his face. "I was only trying to do good. I only wanted to do the right thing."

"You've hurt a child?" I said, making sure I was understanding things.

He only nodded his head. Had I heard a sob?

"Do you need to a lawyer?"

Angry, Will raised his head and pulled his hands away from his face. His expression contorted and now had a look of hatred. Had I blown his trust?

"A lawyer? You think I need a lawyer? What kind of person do you think I am? You think I would do something illegal?" He grimaced and his eyes widened. I had hurt his feelings. Now I felt guilty. I hated hurting people, especially the vulnerable.

"Will, I didn't mean to hurt you, but I'm unclear what has happened. Why don't you help me understand by starting the story from the beginning?"

The rage left his face and sadness replaced it. His eyes clouded as they reflected his personal pain. The young man took several slow, deep breaths. His eyes were directed toward me but they almost seemed to be looking at something else. He was seeing something that he was not looking at. I waited, holding on to my composure as I struggled with the anxiety of silence. When he was ready, he began.

"Two years ago, shortly after I arrived here, a new family came into our congregation. The family was dysfunctional— one that no church wants to deal with, but one that Jesus would want us to minister to. I don't know quite how to describe them. One woman said that they looked like a family that one might find on a PBS documentary of hillbillies."

He paused, as he once again picked up his mug and clutched it as if he was a child with a stuffed animal. The coffee was probably cold by now, but he didn't seem to care. He took a sip, resumed clutching it, and began again.

"Most of our folks wanted to be nice to them but had trouble doing it. They, especially the mother, were loud and unkempt, overbearing and rude. The mother was large. I don't mean just fat, although she was, she was also a large-boned woman with a very big frame. She stood over six feet tall and even if she were thin she would be two hundred pounds. Her size could intimidate people, but not as much as her volume. Her facial features were harsh and not attractive. I heard one of the kids say that she looked the ogre character from 'Shrek.' Some people overcome physical liabilities by having a grand personality. She never developed that ability.

"Her mouth was frequently abusive. The most frequent target of her mouth was her children, but they were not her only victims. She had a few arguments with other mothers. They claimed that her daughter stole whenever she was at another's house to play. It was not long before she and her children were outcasts from the community of young mothers and children."

He paused, collecting his thoughts. The office got deathly quiet. I shifted uncomfortably in my chair and sipped my coffee. The quiet lifted as Will began to compose himself by breathing deeply and loudly. I controlled my anxiety at the near total quiet by tensing and relaxing my calf muscles. I repeated this until he once again began to speak.

"Her husband is chronically depressed and under a doctor's care for that. I have heard a number of people tell the joke that he is depressed because he is married to her. He works for the DPW driving trucks, and makes a lot of overtime money. Many folks have wondered if he works that many hours just to avoid his wife."

Will stopped again to collect his thoughts. I could almost hear the gears of his mind turn as he contemplated where to continue his story.

"I need to tell you about these kids," he finally began. It seemed to me like an eternity, but in reality it was probably only a minute. "The oldest two are adopted. Don't ask me how anyone would allow this couple to adopt. No one in their right mind would have let this couple adopt, but somehow they were allowed. One they adopted is a child with Down syndrome. They adopted her as an infant; she is now fourteen years old but has the mentality of a six-year-old. She is kind-hearted and friendly. Somehow her heart is untainted by the abuse."

He paused, sipped his coffee, and reached for his first cruller of the morning. I had already finished two of them and was debating a third. He ate it in two mouthfuls. This I took as a good sign. He always seemed to be able to eat enormously but gained no weight. I was happy to see him eating again.

"The child always hid. I can guess why. If she wasn't being watched, or with someone, she simply would disappear and we would all scramble to find her. Usually she would be found in a closet or behind furniture but a few times she was outside. Our church property is near a busy street. This was dangerous and had us all worried.

"Whenever this would happen, the mother would begin screaming at the child and haul all three kids into the car to drive them toward home. You could see her screaming at them as they drove away, although once the windows were closed we couldn't hear the abusive lecture. I had a good idea what was being said.

"Shortly after the family transferred to our church and I saw this behavior, I contacted the minister of the church from where they came. It was another Reformed church, and I knew the minister from our college days. I asked him about the family. What he told me was not amusing."

He paused and shifted in his seat. I rose to walk to the coffee pot to fill my mug and pour more into his. He lifted his cup as I filled it. After I returned the mug and sat back down, he continued.

"He told me that the reason the family left his church was because of a birthday party. During the party, the oldest girl disappeared. The joy of the party ended as everyone scrambled to find her. They found her in a wardrobe. The mother was so angry she began shaking the child and screaming 'you f-ing retard, you ruined this party. I should have left you in the retard home and never adopted you.' The kids were horrified and all told their mothers. When the minister spoke to the woman the following week she left the church and fled. Soon she was in my church, spreading her angry poison."

He sipped at his mug and then continued with his story. "The middle child, also adopted, is bright and a thief. Whatever house she would be a guest in would be missing money and jewelry. We think she stole small portable tape recorders from the church as well. This girl looks just like her mother's cousin. Both women deny it but many of us think that she is really the cousin's daughter. On the surface she seems the most adjusted but underneath she, I'm afraid, is headed toward a jail cell.

"Somehow the woman got pregnant, even though doctors said that she would not be able to. She bore a son. The other kids are afraid of him. He talks about enjoying killing rats and cats. I spoke to his mother about this, and she accused the other kids of lying about her boy. We were in her house. She summoned the boy downstairs. He looked scared in front of his mother and denied that he had ever said such things. From the look in his eyes I was convinced that he had said exactly what I had heard that he said."

I felt a knot form in my stomach as I listened to this account. Images of a future serial killerd flashed in front of my face. Was the next Ted Bundy being formed in a Reformed church? I shuddered at the thought.

"Finally, the confrontation came that I knew would eventually come. It had to come. Like a cruise missile that has been launched, it must land at some point. This missile had been launched the minute that this family had arrived at the church. The mother applied to be a volunteer counselor at our Reformed church camp. I could not allow that. She needed a pastoral reference to do so. I began a conversation with her, trying to discourage her from applying. I reminded her of all the times that she had lost her temper with her own kids. She minimized the incidents, accusing people of gossiping and lying about her. Finally, I told her that I could not recommend her to be a counselor. She rose, looking angry, and told me that as a church member she expected a good reference from me."

"I felt that I had no choice. I called the camp director—"

"Dean?" I interrupted. Dean had been camp director for more than a decade, a popular icon in our regional group of churches, and well known for his good judgment.

"Yes, Dean. I told him of my fears and described some of the behavior that I had seen. He thanked me and assured me that he would not have her as a counselor with the kids.

"The woman's reaction was swift and predictable. I received a letter from her within a few days withdrawing her church membership and the membership of her family. I wasn't surprised."

Will paused and tears welled up in his eyes. His body began to shake as if he was reliving a nightmare. He stared at the floor. I fought my urge to push him on, and let him tell his story at his own pace. I rolled my mug back and forth between my palms. I waited—not well, but I waited. He was wordless for two full minutes; it seemed like two full weeks. Finally, he was ready to tell me the real reason he was here.

"The same day that I received the letter from the mother, the middle child called me. It wasn't a pleasant conversation. 'You bastard,' she said to me. 'You took away my only safe place. My mother treats me better at church than anywhere else. I don't have that place now. Do you know what it's like living with her and having no safe place? I hope you die and go to hell.' She hung up after that. What have I done to that kid?"

My stomach cramped and hurt as I heard his rendition. I felt for him. Tears were in his eyes, but he was still bottling up his sadness and hurt. He was letting out sadness, but not enough.

I stood to my full height. "Put your mug down," I commanded. He looked startled, but set his mug on the table. Next I picked him up—my arm behind his knees, my other arm cradling his head in the crook of my elbow, my forearm behind his back, my hand under his arm. He looked shocked as I picked him up.

"Cry," I commanded. "Cry. Let it out. Don't hold this in. Cry, damn it."

He cried and wailed, the hurt, sadness, and anger finding the exhaust that it needed.

3

Assembling a Circle

After Will composed himself, I set him on his feet. "You did the right thing, Will. You protected a cabin full of kids. You, and they, will never know what abuse you saved them from. You are their hero. You showed courage. Thank you for doing this."

"I don't feel much like a hero. I hurt a child," he said.

"I know, but we will work on that. You need to stay here while I make some phone calls. You OK with that?" He only nodded in response. "Come on to the conference room. Relax in the recliner. I'll get you at lunch time. Does your wife know any of this?"

"Not specifics. She knows I'm a bit blue but doesn't know why."

"You have any appointments tomorrow or Saturday?"

"No, just sermon work."

"Book all day Saturday with me. I'm taking you on a trip."

"A trip?"

"Yes, a trip. I'll tell you about it later." I paused to open the door. "Come on. Sit in the recliner and relax." He followed me through the doorway.

The classis office was housed in a building that was once a small independent church. It hadn't lasted long. What was a small sanctuary that probably could not hold more than thirty people was now the reception/waiting room. We walked past Helen's desk, over the hardwood floors in need of refinishing, and through the narrow hallway. Two old Sunday school rooms that now held offices for other part-time staffers lined the hallway.

At the end, on the right, was the conference room, dominated by one large table with wooden chairs around it. It had been formerly used by the old church board of trustees. On the far wall were two reclining chairs with a table and lamp in between. These chairs had comforted other ministers over the years.

"Pick a chair, Will," I said as I opened the door beneath the lamp table and took out a knitted afghan. He sat in the chair on the right; I handed him a pillow and covered him with the blanket. "Get some sleep. I'll stop back." I left the back room and walked back up the hallway.

"Is Will going to be all right?" Helen asked.

"Yes, but please check on him every so often." She smiled and nodded in reply. She had seen other wounded ministers in her tenure and often nurtured them back into health, using a skill set that I envied. "Helen, do you need me for anything? I have some phone calls to make."

"I'm set for now," she smiled, knowing what I would do next.

"Thanks."

I walked back into my office, the former minister's study but now with a solid glass door instead of the old solid wood door—another accommodation to the modern world. Old ministers' studies had solid wood doors for confidentiality. Now, to avoid appearances of impropriety, we used glass to protect ourselves. It was harder for a minister to misbehave, or for someone to lodge false accusations, if your life was lived under glass. I referred to it as "aquarium ministry."

It was ten minutes before I could begin making my phone calls. I simply sat at my desk, with my head in my hands and my eyes closed, grieving for Will, understanding his pain. He was wounded, and somehow by God's grace I hoped to be a catalyst for his healing. Finally, I was ready to call. I grabbed my Rolodex to look for the first number. My young colleagues often tease me about my Rolodex, and urge me to keep my numbers electronically—at the same time they urge the nation to use less energy. My Rolodex is energy-efficient, even "green," and never needs a battery charge. It works.

I called Ginny de Plore first; she answered on the first ring. Did she know where he was? Was she sitting by the phone waiting?

"Ginny, Jack Berg, how are you doing?"

"I'm fine, thank you. You must be calling for Will. He's not here now."

"He's with me now, Ginny, in the office. He's having a tough time, as you know. I'm trying to help him." Did I hear a sigh of relief?

"He's OK? I didn't know where he was."

"He came here to talk. He's pretty hurt by a problem with a church family. I'm taking him on a retreat on Saturday with a few other ministers. I imagine he will stay here for the rest of today. Does that work for you?"

"Yes, thank you. I've been worried about him."

"What have you seen that makes you worry?"

She paused for a moment. I looked out the window, needing a distraction from the silent pause. I looked at two squirrels frolicking at the base of a pine tree.

"Two days ago, everything seemed normal when he went to the office, but he hasn't been right since he came home. Something happened during the day. He has been quiet and brooding ever since and simply tells me that he 'can't talk about it.' His mood has me worried."

"He is in good hands, Ginny. I'll have him call you after lunch. OK?"

"That's fine. Thank you, Jack." I hung up the phone, glad to bring the woman some relief.

My next call was to Dean. A Midwesterner like myself, he grew up on a farm in South Dakota, but unlike me he did not love that life. He loved the woods, not the pastures, and at one time was enrolled in seminary. He and his professors questioned whether or not he was called to ministry, and he quit in his second semester to become associate director of our conference center, housed in woods in the Hudson Valley of New York. Since then he has risen to being director.

A tall, round, man with a large belly and a bushy black beard, he looked something like Grizzly Adams—indeed, that was his nickname for some; others called him Black Beard. He loved beef, laughed at vegans, and was more politically conservative than one would expect in a mainline church. He would offend a lot of people if not for his gift of hospitality. Now, after a decade, he was an icon. Hundreds of youth moving into leadership in our congregations loved him and would follow him to the ends of the earth.

I got the conference center answering machine on my first attempt, and left a message. I tried his cell, and got through.

"Hey, Jack, good morning."

"Hello, Dean. Things well by you?"

"No complaints. What may I do for you?"

Dean had many quirks, one of which was that he would never ask, "What can I do for you?" He insisted that it was better grammar to ask, "What may I do for you?" Somehow it mattered to Dean.

"I need a retreat house for possibly seven people on Saturday. You have something available?

"That is short notice, Jack."

"I know, but something came up. Is it possible?"

"I can give you the Calvin Lodge, but I need you out in time to clean it for a group coming at nine for a sleepover."

"That will work out fine. Thanks. I'll make sure that we leave it in good condition."

"I know, Jack. What time are you arriving?"

"Hopefully by ten."

"I'll have it ready by eight."

"Thanks, Dean."

With a place, date, and time secured, I was free to make calls to the other five ministers I was inviting—not so much inviting as demanding, as much as my office *could* demand.

My first call was to Madeline Bell, a minister in her thirties serving her first congregation. "Hello," she answered with the most pleasant, however slight, French accent. Madeline was French Canadian by birth and had grown up Catholic, as had most folks of French origin. A very pious and religious child who had been educated in Catholic schools since kindergarten, she desired to be the first female priest in Montreal. Her mistake was that she mentioned this dream to an elderly nun who taught religious studies. The nun not only castigated her but also recruited a few priests to assist with correcting her. They came on strong; she described it as "abusive." The nun and the priests had found a way to drive a most pious child from their church. Madeline found her way into the Presbyterian Church of Canada, and finally into the Reformed Church in America. She was a great addition.

"Maddy, it's Jack. Do you have a minute?"

"Of course, but let me tell you now that I'm already doing two classis committees and I don't have time for more." She paused. "Now, what do you want to talk about?" I chuckled at her directness. She claimed it was her French background that gave her this assertiveness. Whatever the reason, I always found it to be rather refreshing, among ministers who usually don't speak their true feelings and hold resentments and/or give themselves ulcers.

"No committees. I need a circle meeting. One of our colleagues is in trouble."

"When and where? You know I will be there."

"Thanks, Madeline. Saturday at the retreat center at ten."

"Do I need to bring anything?"

"No. I'll bring everything; just please, be there."

"I will. Count on me."

"Thanks, Madeline."

I next called Walter Blanco, one of the few Latinos from our area who had grown up in the Reformed Church. His parents, middle-class Cubans, had been members of one of the larger Reformed churches in New York City. Once they moved to New Jersey they found the nearest Reformed church, where Walter was baptized. Now forty years old, Walter had recently founded his third Spanish-speaking congregation in our classis. He was an asset I was glad to have.

His phone went to voice mail on the third ring. "Walter, this is Jack. I need a circle meeting at the Calvin House on Saturday at ten. Please let me know if you can make it. You don't need to bring anything but yourself. I hope you can come. A brother needs our help."

I placed the phone onto the cradle and looked for the number for Harvey Grumm, the oldest active minister in our classis. A social worker by trade, he entertained many young ministers with stories of his days as a social worker during the race riots of the 1960s. Perhaps it was a legend, perhaps it was true, but he claimed that his relations with the black community were good enough for him to be the only white man allowed into the black sections of Newark at the height of the riots. He entered what the police called the "war zone," in order to check on the welfare of an elderly lady who was one of his cases.

Always a ruling elder of his congregation, he entered seminary following his mandatory retirement from the county welfare system, and became the minister of social justice at his home church. He was unpaid but didn't care. He lived off his government pension and did what he enjoyed doing.

"Harvey, it's Jack; I need a favor."

"Of course, you need a favor. You only call when you need a favor," he answered in his standard, gruff voice. "When are you coming to see our ministry here? It's been a while."

"I was there two Sundays ago, Harvey. They told me you were sick; that's why you weren't there."

"Yeah, I had the flu. No one told me you were here. I'm sorry. What can I do for you?"

"I need a meeting of our circle. A minister is in trouble."

"When and where, Jack? I'll be there."

"I knew you would. I appreciate your loyalty. Saturday at ten at the Calvin House."

"Count on me."

"I'll see you there."

"Why didn't you people tell me that Jack was here . . ." he was saying as he hung up the phone. I had seen him show temper a few times and didn't envy his office staff.

I looked up Laura Heffner's number next. Now a ten-year veteran of ministry, Laura was born in the wrong generation. She looked like the hippies of my generation. She stood six feet tall and had blond hair to her waist. She had a small part-time church, ran a cottage industry quilting and doing stained glass, and lived mostly from the royalties from the fashion modeling that she had done in her youth. She still held her good looks, and most of the men of the classis hoped to serve on committees with her. She was one of the most creative and artistic ministers whom I had ever met.

"Hello," she said into the telephone over laughter. I didn't know what she was laughing at, or with whom, but it really was not any of my business. "I'm sorry," she said, her laughter ending, "may I help you?"

"This is Jack, Laura. Do you have a minute?"

"Sure, what's up? Is it confidential? Should I clear the room?"

"What is going on over there?"

"I'm just chatting with a dog breeder. I'm thinking of starting a new business of breeding Labs."

"You need another business?"

"I can't help it. Sometimes these businesses just find me. I can be a midwife to canines. Something about that sounds sacred." I closed my eyes and shook my head as I tried not to laugh. Laura did what Laura did. One appreciated her or scorned her. I have yet to meet someone with a neutral opinion of her.

"I have something else sacred for you, Laura. A minister needs healing and I need a circle meeting. I don't want to describe details but I'm calling a circle meeting for Saturday at ten at the retreat center."

"Can you pick me up? My truck is in the shop." This wasn't much of a request. Her home was on the way for me.

"No problem, Laura. Why don't I pick you up around half past eight?"

"OK, but also, I have two special order quilts to finish. I'll need to bring them with me to work on."

"Your quilts are fine, Laura. I'll pick you up."

"You bringing soy milk or should I bring my own?"

"I'll bring some."

"Thanks, Jack. I'll see you then."

My final call was to Ralph Vanden Oot, one of the youngest ministers of our area. He was every Dutch mother's dream, standing six-foot-four with blond hair and clear blue eyes. He grew up in Western Michigan and went to Reformed church college and seminary, but had done an internship in the east and had fallen in love with the New York City area. He never went back. His first call was short and ended badly. Now in his second congregation, he seemed to have found his footing.

"This is Pastor Ralph," the phone machine informed me, "leave a message following the tone."

"Ralph, this is Jack Berg. Please call me—"

"This is Ralph," he said, interrupting my message. "What's up, Jack?"

I explained and he agreed to be there.

I breathed a little easier, now that my Saturday plans were made. I needed only to hear from Walter, but even without him we had enough to complete a circle. I felt pleased and a bit relieved. If any group could help Will, it was this circle. They were talented and sensitive. They were full of the Holy Spirit and natural healers. God had given me a great gift with the presence of this group, and this weekend they would show their gifts and talents.

I left my office, and walked past Helen to check on Will. What I saw pleased me. He was asleep in the recliner under a blanket. I stood in the doorway for a few moments, grateful that he was calm enough to sleep. I hoped that his dreams were peaceful. My cell phone interrupted me with a beep, informing me of a text message. It was from Walter.

"I'll be there, Chief," was all it said.

"Thank you, God," was all I could think.

I stared down at the phone for a few minutes while I collected my thoughts. This, like many days, was not the day that I had anticipated when I had opened the office this morning. I was happy that the circle members were on board, but now I needed to make my preparations.

"Prepare, prepare, prepare," my grandfather had always taught us on the farm, "unless you want to go to bed hungry this winter." Every fall as we harvested vegetables, we carefully canned in Ball jars a portion of our harvested vegetables for the winter and stored them in the fruit cellar. It was a job that I hated. The animal part of farming I enjoyed, but the vegetable activities bored me. Grandpa encouraged me along with his reminder to "prepare, prepare, prepare." I appreciate the lessons of preparedness, but vegetable gardening still has no appeal to me.

My next call was to my wife's cell phone. I knew that she wouldn't be able to answer but I wanted to leave a message for her. "Ruth, it's Jack. I'm going to be busy on Saturday morning and I wanted to give you a heads-up. I'll be back early evening, so we can plan something for then. I'm sorry about this but it can't be helped."

I hung up, knowing that I had better be coming home tonight with flowers. I grabbed a piece of scrap paper, really a half sheet of paper taken from first drafts of printing, from my pile and the first item I wrote on it was "one dozen red roses." This was part of the all-important domestic defense of marriage.

I then took a few minutes to complete my shopping list for the weekend. It was then that Ruth sent a text to me: "I understand, but you still owe me."

My clock struck half past eleven, and I felt that it was time to check on Will. I opened my door and walked past Helen, who was eating one of her many apples. She seemed to never be without one during the day.

I passed her desk and returned up the hall to check on Will. He was only half-asleep now, stirring and moving his legs as part of his wake-up sequence.

"Will, you awake?"

Bleary-eyed, he picked up his head and looked in my direction.

"Yes, Jack."

"Soon it is lunch time."

"I'm not really hungry, Jack."

"Well, come and talk to me while I eat. I can use the company."

I returned to Helen.

"Don't forget your annual report, Jack, and the annual meeting packet" Helen reminded me.

"I'll make sure it is done before noon tomorrow," I said, although I knew that this meant a very late night of work that would cost me another dozen roses. "I'm off to lunch with Will. Please call me with any emergencies."

Will and I had lunch at a local place owned by a man I knew well enough to request a private table in the back. We didn't talk about the issue at hand. Instead we kept it light, sharing amusing stories from past, happier times. By the end of our time he was even laughing a bit.

I followed him home in my car to make sure he arrived safely and in the arms of his wife. I visited with them for an hour and reminded he and Ginny that he would be away with me all day Saturday. I arranged to pick him up at eight. I wanted to make sure that he got there and back. Finally, satisfied that these two would be all right until tomorrow I rose to take my leave. Ginny hugged me in the doorway with grateful affection. I returned the hug and went on my way.

"Thank you, Jack," Ginny said with a pained smile.

"You're welcome."

At last I was on the road again, on the way back to the office to the tasks that were at hand. Helen kept me on task. My life never ran on a straight line from point A to point B. There were always too many unexpected events and too many urgent events to allow that. Every year I made sure I showed Helen my appreciation on Administrative Assistant's Day.

On the way back to the office, I called Ruth to let her know that I would be late and not to hold dinner for me. If she was disappointed, her voice did not betray her. Maybe it was all the years of seeing me called out on emergencies that had trained her. Maybe she was just born to be a minister's wife. Maybe it was a little of both. Whatever the reason, she was understanding and a real blessing to my ministry.

It took me almost three hours to finish my report and mark corrections in the annual meeting packet. Finally, I was finished. It was almost ten o'clock and I felt weary from the day. It wasn't the physical pain that tired me but the emotional pain. My body ached to take away the pain that Will was feeling. It was something I have struggled with since I began ministry—owning the pain of others. The mentors I had in my early years of ministry helped me to control it, but it was always there waiting to invade my spirit. I struggled now to keep the pain away, to help Will without owning pain that did not belong to me.

Slowly I rose from my desk, turned out the lights, and locked the doors. My trip home was quick; I made one stop at the late-night grocery to pick up two dozen roses for Ruth. Finally, my day was complete. I looked forward to her company and a much-needed sleep in preparation for tomorrow.

4

The Depressed and the Hippie

It was 7:45 when I pulled my car into Will's driveway Saturday morning. The Tudor-style house sat on a block of similar houses that had once housed Protestants moving out of Hudson County, during the post-World War II exodus from the more urbanized areas. Now Orthodox Jews occupied the neighborhood and much of the small town. The congregation that Will served had diminished, and it could barely afford full-time ministry. He and his wife must be worried over their futures and their financial security. Losing one family could have a large effect on such a small group.

I knew that I was early. I was always early. I always came before appointed times. In my mind, being late showed disrespect for the agreed-upon meeting time. I could always wait for things to begin, but if you were late you could never make up for missing a beginning. I sat in the car and prepared to wait, when the house door popped open and Ginny poked her head out.

"Come in, Jack. I have coffee on."

I left the car and followed her into the kitchen, smelling the brewed coffee as I walked.

"How is he?" I asked, doubting that anything had changed since I spoke to him on the phone yesterday.

"About the same. He is moping and quiet. Jack, have you ever once seen him quiet?"

"No. Never. That is what scares me."

"You know, in college he once had a bet with his frat brothers that he could remain quiet for an hour. He lost the bet." She laughed out loud, and I laughed with her.

"Why did he take the bet?

"I don't know. Maybe he wasn't self-aware then."

"It is good to hear you laugh, Ginny."

She walked toward me and put her hands on my upper arms. Tears welled in her eyes.

"Will you make him laugh again? Will you please? I want our kids to hear his wonderful laugh. Jack, make it happen, please." She held me close now and sobbed.

"I'll try, Ginny. I'll do my best."

She unclutched me, turned to the stove, and wiped her tears away before pouring coffee into a mug and handing it to me. I thanked her; she did not respond but instead simply turned away and tried to compose herself.

For the next couple minutes, we mostly stood in silence. She looked at the floor, as I coped with the lack of noise by sipping from the cup. Finally, I could hear the footsteps of Will descending the stairs. I turned to greet him.

"How are you, Will?"

He shrugged his shoulders before answering, "I guess OK."

"That is better than a few days ago."

"I suppose."

Ginny handed him a travel mug of coffee, kissed him goodbye, and walked us to the door. She shut the door behind us and we walked to the car.

Will remained silent as we pulled out of the driveway and began our drive toward the highway to pick up Laura. She lived in a rural area eighteen miles from Will's suburban town. In New Jersey, we calculate travel not by miles but by time—during rush hour, that distance could take an hour and a half. Fortunately, it was Saturday morning and the malls would not be open for two more hours; the eighteen miles could be covered rather quickly on such a morning. We cruised along in silence, neither of us knowing what to say.

It was almost 8:30 when we pulled up in front of Laura's house. It looked like an old farmhouse. Laura had it decorated with homemade macramé dream-catchers that hung from the beams of the wraparound porch. A flag hung from the porch proclaimed, "Love your mother," with a picture of the Earth in the background. Three dogs of mixed varieties ran around the yard between the porch and the fence. They barked a warm welcome until Laura opened the door, called a greeting to us, and whistled the dogs back into the house.

"I wish my kids obeyed me like her dogs obey her," Will quipped.

I chuckled, happy at his show of humor. "It is hard to say 'no' to her. She is charismatic with high energy. Most of all, she is a loveable nonconformist."

"I have never met her," said Will. "I have seen her at events but I have never been introduced to her or spoken to her."

"You are in for an experience."

"Is that . . . good?"

"More than that."

A minute later the house door opened, and Laura exited with three large canvas shopping bags. She turned and squatted as the dogs came to the doorway. She received a goodbye kiss from each of them before they retreated into the house.

Laura walked her tall, willowy body toward us as though she was walking down a catwalk. She was dressed in a tie-dye wraparound skirt down to her ankles, and a plain white sleeveless top. She wore a Celtic cross around her neck, held by hemp cord that was the perfect length to allow the cross to hang into her larger than average bosom. Her long blonde hair, hanging down below her waistline, framed her beautiful smile. I got out of the car to open the door for her.

"Jack, good to see you. How are you?" She set her bags on the ground, and hugged and kissed me before I could even answer her.

"Fine, Laura, how are things?"

"Really good. I saw my first butterfly of the season this morning. I was on the back porch enjoying the morning with my green tea, and the first one hovered in, checking out the plants coming up. I always know God's presence when the birds and butterflies come by. Yesterday I spent all morning watching a robin. What a beautiful yard."

She paused her descriptions just long enough to pick up her bags. "I brought hummus, tofu, and soy milk, just in case you forgot."

"I bought those, Laura."

"Better too much than too little. Whatever we don't use I'll bring home."

She paused and turned to look at Will through the car window. Their eyes locked and her face changed. I had the impression that she was feeling his emotions. She set her bags once again and reached her hand into the car.

"I'm Laura," she said.

"Will," he said, taking her hand.

"I'm so sorry. You are in great pain." Laura extended her left hand through the window to take Will's into both of hers. Their eyes locked as she held on, as if she could draw his pain out of him. If she could, I wonder where she would store it. "We will make it better."

She let him go, picked up her bags, and climbed into the back seat.

"You want the front?" Will asked. "You have the longer legs."

"No, thank you. I'll be fine. You two talk. I didn't finish my morning meditation." After arranging the bags on the seat next to her, she shut the door and waited until I was back in the car. "Just leave me alone for a while, please, Jack. I need to get grounded."

"Not a problem, Laura. Let me know when you are ready to converse."

"I will. I promise."

In the corner of my eye I could see Will smirking, wanting to laugh but not wishing to be rude. This was his first real experience with Laura. An encounter with Laura changes everyone.

I backed out of the driveway and rolled toward the highway. Laura was already sitting with her hands on her knees, palms up, with her eyes closed and meditating with deep, regular breathing.

I began the final half-hour drive to the retreat house with two silent companions. Will stared at the road, deep in thought, while Laura rested in the deep recesses of her mind. The two were more at peace than I was, as I had no sound but the sound of tires on the road. I kept my mind busy to overlook the silence. I ran through my grocery list, reminding myself that I had not forgotten anything. I ran through my introduction to the group that I would give to Will. In short, I did everything I could to make sure I didn't know that all was quiet.

5

Assembled Circle

The final half-mile was on a dirt road. It seemed to be a contradiction, being just twenty-two miles north of the Empire State Building, but there we were. Not a word had been spoken since we had left Laura's house. I fought my anxiety, riding on the dirt among the pine trees, until we came to the clearing and Calvin House.

Calvin House was the newest of the small retreat houses at the camp and used mostly for church groups and small youth gatherings. Built mostly by volunteers from around the classis, it had all the modern kitchen conveniences but was made to look rustic, with shiplap siding and wooden roof shingles. Except for the barrier-free ramp and the ten-car parking lot, the outside looked as if it had been built one hundred years before.

I had fond memories of this cabin. I'd used it to meet with new ministers in the classis, and had held retirement dinners here for those on the other end of ministry. Several youth groups had asked me to lead retreats for them here. Several of our circle meetings had been held here, including the first. This was a sacred place.

Four cars sat in the lot, corresponding with the four circle members standing in front of the cabin. They stood quietly outside, guarding this house of healing. I looked at the dashboard clock and saw that I was five minutes late. My stomach churned. I hated being late.

A loud sigh from the back seat interrupted my self-deprecating thoughts, as Laura had come out of her meditation at the same time as I drove into the small parking lot. Was it providence, luck, or was it simply a choice that she made upon hearing the change of the pavement sound?

I parked the car, exited, and inhaled deeply as I smelled the soothing odor of the pine trees. They were refreshing, reminding me of the pleasant scent of Christmas. I wished that this day would fill me with such pleasant memories. I nodded silently to the four who waited at the door and they returned the silent greetings.

Will sat in the car not knowing what to do, his anxiety growing by the minute. The silent watchers of the group did nothing to alleviate his stress. They were as silent as if they were attending a wake, as they stood guarding the building and mostly staring at the ground. Laura opened the door for Will and beckoned to him. He hesitated before turning and standing. She held his arm and began to walk him toward the others. He walked with his head facing down, allowing her arm to hold him in comfort. I was reminded of a lioness protecting a wounded cub.

She walked him to the group. Very softly, each one made an introduction and the seven of us stood for a moment in silence. I broke the silence. "It is time to carry in our supplies."

They followed me to the trunk and lined up. Walter—tall, blond, and strong—was the first in line. His youth and strength was a great asset. I handed him the ice chest filled with the perishable meats and ice. I handed Madeline a canvas bag of communion elements. Ralph stood next; he was short but had very broad shoulders and was an amateur weightlifter. I handed him the two bags of snacks and produce.

"I want the talking stick and the candle, Jack. I feel at peace when I hold them," said Laura, referring to the Christ candle and the stick with four feathers on it that I had received as a gift from an Apache. I couldn't help but see the smirks of the group at Laura's enthusiasm. We all loved Laura, but she never failed to amuse us. I handed her the bag holding the talking stick and the candle. She grabbed it, clutched it to her bosom, and grabbed Will once again as she walked him toward Calvin House.

I picked up the final canvas bag, closed the trunk, and motioned to Harvey, the oldest of us, to follow me. Together we walked up the ramp and through the door. Harvey closed the door behind us. The lights were already on and the work had begun. Whatever talking there was continued very quietly.

Madeline worked with the speed of a professional chef as she and Ralph cut the fruit and cheese, arranging the snacks on large platters. Laura, with Will in tow, was already setting a small, round coffee table in the living room with a circle of seven chairs around it. She placed the candle and the stick in the center of the table. Walter and Harvey had coffee brewing and were preparing split chicken breasts in roasting pans ready to be placed in the oven at the proper time. Next, they washed the potatoes and peeled carrots for the luncheon roast.

Madeline and Ralph had arranged the snacks on snack tables interspersed between chairs. By ones and twos, we gathered, filled plates with finger food, and stood near the common area chairs waiting for us to begin. I looked at the faces of the members. They were all ready. I looked at Will. He was needy.

It was time to begin. I stood at the center of the room next to the table and began the mantra that the group had developed several years ago.

"Do not let your hearts be troubled," I invoked the words of St. John's gospel in my best preaching voice.

"Do not let your hearts be troubled," the five prior members of our group, repeated back to me. Will stood puzzled, not knowing what to do. I began again.

"Do not let your hearts be troubled," I repeated. On cue, the other replied with the same words. It was our way to get group attention.

"Do not let your hearts be troubled," the six others repeated back.

"Trust the father, trust also in me."

The group repeated each of my sentences.

"In my father's house are many rooms."

"If it were not so would I have told you that I go to prepare a place for you?"

"And when I go and prepare a place for you I will come again and take you to myself."

"That where I am you may be also."

"You know the way to the place where I am going."

"But Thomas said to him, 'Lord, we don't know where you are going, how can we know the way?'"

"Jesus said, 'I am the way and the truth and the life, no one gets to the Father except through me.'"

I sat, and the others joined me. Will, clinging to me, sat at my right. Next to him was Laura, clinging to him. The other four selected the chairs closest to where they stood. The circle had begun. I lit the candle, turned toward Will, and began.

"Will, this is a circle meeting. Harvey and I started the first circle meeting five years ago. The circle exists for one purpose and one purpose only: to support and heal its members. Each of us has been wounded. Usually these wounds are from ministry, but not always. We all have been called to ministry and uphold our sacred vows. When we live those calls, we sometimes get hurt."

I paused waiting for the words to sink in. Each member of the circle looked at me and then alternately at Will, making sure that he heard and understood—making sure that he knew that he wasn't alone in his pain. They nervously munched on snacks and sipped juice and water.

"Several of us, Will, have wished death, or planned death, because of these hurts. Our gospel telling is a reminder that only Jesus can decide when it is our time to die. It is not ours to decide. If we die by our own hand, we dishonor Jesus, and hurt a lot of people around us." Again, I paused before continuing.

"There is another lesson, Will. Jesus said these comforting words to a group of disciples, not to individuals. If we walk through ministry alone, we will feel grief and depression. It is with the comfort of others that we have the full power of the Holy Spirit. Stay connected to this circle, Will. My hunch is that you have been a bit of a lone ranger, not nurturing relationships with other ministers. We need each other. We are your support group. Stay connected with us and we will all stay connected with you."

I waited as the group members nodded in affirmation. Will scanned their faces, not knowing quite what to think. This day gave him a lot to take in.

"This," I said, picking up the talking stick sitting on the table, "was a gift to me from an Apache I knew when I was a seminary student. The Apaches have a tribal custom at meetings; whoever held the stick had the privilege of the floor and spoke without interruption from anyone. We will be using this today. Each of us will have a turn using the stick, sharing our stories, and talking about our healing. When we are holding the stick, we will have the attention of everyone, and will not be interrupted."

I stopped. Will looked in rapt attention. The others had heard this before and sat more in anticipation and less in awe.

"We will go in the order of joining this circle, Will. Everyone will get a chance. You will be last and when you are done, we will help you toward healing."

"Since I started the circle, I will begin."

6

She Was Beaten by My Pride

We all sat in our circle, and I began by picking up the stick. Will stared at me in disbelief. "You need the stick?" he asked me.

"More than you can know. There is a reason I founded this circle." I took a breath, drank a bit of coffee, closed my eyes for a moment and began: "I was young once, a bit naive and quite stupid. I wasn't quite what you would call a fundamentalist, but close. I could quote Scripture and tell you what was right and what was wrong, but I had not lived long enough to see how our values and beliefs interacted with the real world. I was prideful and did not listen as well as I might have. I thought that as a minister of the word, surely I could invoke the healings that Jesus did. Other people paid for my pride, and I carry the guilt to this day.

"I began in a small, rural parish full of energy, optimism, and naivety. I toured around the area, introducing myself to the members first and then to the community residents who were nonmembers, inviting them into the fellowship. It was during one of my visits that I met a woman who was not a member, but a neighbor close to the church who seemed very sad. Her name was Diane. She seemed shut down and afraid of her own shadow. Diane was in her late twenties, married with two young children. I visited her and met her children, but her husband was never around when I visited.

"Her home was typical of other homes that I had seen. It was clean but not fancy. Few people in that area had surplus money for decorating or anything else that was not practical. The furniture appeared as though it was all garage-sale purchased. The children were polite, almost too polite. They played together but were quieter than most children. It seemed a bit odd but I didn't think very much of it.

"I visited for perhaps an hour and asked if she wanted me to pray with her. She asked for prayers for strength. She would not elaborate, but told me twice that she wanted prayers for strength. I prayed fervently for her and invited her and her children to church as I left. I never thought that she would. I was surprised when she did.

"The congregation greeted her warmly, and she and her children responded well. Some of the members had seen her in town but none had met her before. They speculated that she was a newer resident. She became a regular for several months and her children became part of the Sunday school. Not unlike other families, she and her children came while her husband did not. The other husbands we had seen occasionally at various events. Diane's husband was a mystery. No one ever recalled seeing him.

"My summer installation was still glowing within me as the fall turned toward Advent and Christmas. Remember now, I was only twenty-five at this time. I was still convinced that if I worked hard, said the right prayers, and spoke nicely to everyone, there was no miracle that I couldn't induce. I was certain that with a bit of prayer and love I could find out the cause of this woman's sadness. In short, I was young and self-assured, thinking that I was a miracle worker.

"It was at the start of Advent that Diane asked to see me during the week. When I suggested an evening, she asked for a daytime appointment based on the children's schedule. We agreed on a morning appointment. I looked forward to the session. Perhaps I could find out what was making her so sad and 'fix' her.

"She arrived at ten in the morning, looking rather tired. Her eyes were puffy, giving me the appearance that she had gotten very little sleep the night before. She gratefully accepted the mug of coffee that I offered her.

"'What did you want to speak to me about?' I asked her.

"'I'm in a dilemma,' she explained. 'My husband has been in jail. Soon he will be released, and I am debating whether to move far away so he cannot find me or the kids.'

"I now understood why no one had ever seen this man, even as my mind raced with all types of scenarios. Was he a mass murderer? Had we seen him on the news? Clearly with children so young, he could not have been in jail for long.

"'What is he incarcerated for?' I asked her.

"'Possession of drugs, but he swears that he wasn't in possession. His friend in the car with him had marijuana and dropped a bag. I believe him. He has never lied to me before.'

"'Are you sure?' I asked.

"Her face showed a bit of resentment. 'Yes,' she said, looking a bit annoyed that I had pushed this point with her.

"'When will he be released?'

"'Two weeks before Christmas.' She rolled her eyes as she said, 'he exhibited good behavior. I wish he showed good behavior before he was arrested.'

"'How had he acted?'

"'He was impatient and could get pretty short-tempered. Things were tense when he was around. This might be a sin, Pastor, but I have really enjoyed having him away.'

"'Does he seem like he has changed?' I asked her.

"'I don't know. He has only written two letters since he was away.'

"'What does he look like during visiting day?' I inquired.

"She dropped her gaze to her lap and her face flushed. 'I haven't seen him.'

"'You never saw him? Not once?'

"Diane dropped her head. I could see tears beginning to sprout. 'No,' she replied. 'I didn't want to see him and I sure wasn't going to bring the kids to a jail.'

"'I'm assuming that he might be angry about that,' I interjected.

"'I don't know,' she told me. 'I guess so. He didn't mention it in his letter but that was a while ago.' She paused and then continued. 'I'm sure that he is clean now. I doubt that he was able to use while he was locked up.'

"'So, he is a user?' I said.

"'He used from time to time but not often. I'm afraid to give him another chance. Things have been peaceful with him gone.'

"'What about your children? Do you really want them to be raised without a father? Being a single mother can't be easy.'

"'It isn't,' Diane told me. 'But I'm not so sure that it is worse than when he was around.'

"'If he is clean, won't he be better to live with than before?'

"'I hope and pray for that, but I'm really doubtful.'

"'Have some hope. Things can change, Diane.'

"'It would take a miracle.'

"'Miracles? We celebrate miracles here.' I smiled at her and she returned it. It was the first time all morning I had seen her smile.

"'So,' she said. 'You really think that I should stay with him?'

"'Yes, I do. You took wedding vows to be with him always. I believe that we need to take wedding vows seriously. I believe that you should be faithful to him.'

"'I'll try, I really will,' she said, looking very disappointed. This was clearly not the response that she was hoping for. She rose, thanked me, set her coffee cup down, and left the office.

"Diane continued to attend church but she seemed depressed and withdrawn. Advent began and the joy I felt at celebrating my first Christmas season as a pastor was tempered with my worry about Diane. I wondered if she really would try to make a good marriage with her husband.

"When I look back at this point in my life I feel pretty embarrassed. I was naïve. I thought that an unmarried man knew enough to give advice on how to be married. I grew up in a region that had very little substance abuse, and certainly in my straitlaced family I had no personal experience with it. I really thought that I could give good advice to a woman who was living with a substance abuser, even though I didn't. I was a bit of a fundamentalist back in those days and very proud of my biblical knowledge. I knew that the Bible forbids divorce, and that was the end of the story for me. Diane paid a horrible price for her own bad judgment, as well as my inept advice.

"It was ten days before Christmas when I received a call from the county police. Diane was found beaten and unconscious along the road several miles from her house. She had no identification with her. She had a folded bulletin from our church in her back pocket. The police asked me to come to the hospital to identify her. As I drove that night being asked to identify a 'Jane Doe,' my gut told me that it might be Diane. My mind whirled, my heart pounded, and my stomach felt sick. I quickly made the identification, and vomited as I saw the bruising and stitches. My guilt deepened. I drove to her house, following the police. We were concerned about the safety of her children and the whereabouts of her husband.

"No one was home when we arrived. A search began for him and the kids. The young ones were found two days later in the home of relatives of their father. Child Protective Services allowed them to stay with the relatives rather than foster care. The husband was not found until several days after that, as he hid in an apartment of a crack house in Schenectady.

"The police shocked me by telling me that Diane earned money as an exotic dancer at a local bar. Until they found her husband, and he confessed, their two theories were that she was attacked by him or that she was attacked by a bar customer.

"For three days, I visited Diane at her bedside and prayed over her unconscious body. Because she danced for a living, I visited her with a bad attitude. I was compensating for my guilt and looking down upon her with a bit of self-righteousness. I prayed for her, but I was going through the motions. I did not feel the same love and compassion for her that I once felt. In short, I was acting as a Pharisee, not as a servant of Christ.

"Diane woke from being unconscious after three days. She seemed happy to see me. I was her only visitor. She also looked angry. It was hard for her to speak through her cuts and bruises. The only news that she really wanted was to know that her husband was in jail and that her children were safe.

"After a week, she went home from the hospital and reclaimed her kids. She was out of work until her face healed enough to allow makeup to cover her bruises. I made sure that our deacon's fund contributed to her children's Christmas presents.

"I must admit that my first Christmas as a pastor was a time of conflicted emotions. Christmas was a joy. I left late at night, after Christmas Eve service, to spend the day with my family. My thoughts always went back to Diane and her injuries. her children knowing their father was in jail and seeing the results of domestic violence. I know that my advice contributed to this evil. Joy and guilt both lived within me.

"My family worried about me but I never let on what was happening. Christmas was good, but not as good as it would have been. The glow of ministry, within six months, felt tarnished.

"The new year came, but Diane did not. She stayed away, resuming the life that she had known before accepting my invitation to the church. I wondered if she would have been better off if she had never heard of the church or me.

"I spent the better part of Lent reaching out to her, but she never let go of her pain and her resentment against me. Several of the church ladies visited her, but even they could not persuade her to return. Diane and her children were lost to us.

"So where does a minister go to get pastoral care? We had no such thing as Classis Executives back then. That is a much more recent invention. There was, however, an older, seemingly kind minister in our classis based in a congregation not very far away from me. I went to see him. Perhaps he could show me a way to get Diane back and demonstrate ways to get rid of guilt.

"I walked into David's office. He greeted me and beckoned to sit in one of his overstuffed leather chairs. He sat across from me and lit his pipe, making no small talk. He sat sucking on his old pipe as he looked at me.

"'What's on your mind, Jack?'

"I told him the story, as he looked at me with a blank expression. Finally, when I was done, he shocked me with his reaction.

"'Jack, why are you trying to get that girl back in church? Do you think so little of your congregation that you would want a strip dancer in it? Are they teaching you people anything in seminary nowadays?'

"'David,' I interrupted, 'She is a young woman getting beaten and struggling to raise two kids by herself. She needs our support.'

"'Jack, you're young and I like you, but let me explain to you how life works. God is just and people get what they deserve. This young girl lived an immoral life. She married a drug addict. She's getting her punishment. Don't fret so much about it.'

"'David, do you really mean this? A woman was beaten.'

"'I know that, Jack, but she contributed to her misery. Jack, we are called to righteousness. When we act unrighteously, we get punished. Let her go. If she repents at some point, then let her back in. She'd only be a bad example for the others if she came back now.'

"David continued on in his diatribe while I sat uncomfortably listening to him. I realized that if I continued along my prideful way I would sound just like him in ten years. That was the day I opened my heart and decided to be a lover, not a moralist.

"Diane never came back. I never saw her children again. I never met her husband. Even though I've worked on establishing safe congregations for all, I have still carried guilt. Finally, one day I found a way to use that guilt as a way of being a catalyst to help others. Ten years after meeting Diane I met Harvey, when he planned to kill himself, and I shared with him my soul.

"Thus, began our circle."

I set the stick down.

7

Baby Killer

I looked at Harvey, as I called on him to share his story. He dropped his eyes and took several deep breaths. Such meetings were difficult on all of us. We were called upon to remember things that we would rather not remember. After a few moments, he picked up the talking stick in his old hands, wiped a tear from his eye, and began his story.

"Will, I wanted to kill myself. God knows I deserved it. God had other plans and he sent Jack to prevent it. I am here because of him. Perhaps it would have been more merciful had I been allowed to die. My guilt would have died with me. Instead, I live, and not a day goes by that I do not feel shame.

"I was born just before World War II began. Everyone went to church back then; it was part of what America was. I'm not sure that everyone who went to church was always a Christian but they went to church, at least.

"I enjoyed church; it was a place away from my father, who was a mean drunk. My mother put up with my father, his drinking, and his violence. Back then there weren't too many options for women. There were few anti-poverty programs then. Some church people helped us out a bit. There were times that we depended on the deacon's fund. We were loyal and faithful members, and the deacons seemed happy to help us.

"I was the golden boy of church. I attended every worship service and every social event. My Sunday school teachers and the minister all told me that I ought to go to seminary. I resisted the call to ministry. I hated being told what to do. This is a side effect of my growing up with abusive authority. I didn't trust authority and actively resisted it. The more church members told me that I should go to seminary the less I considered it as an option.

"I was ten when my baby brother was born, as a result of one of the many reconciliations my parents had after my father would promise to never to be near a bar again. I did a lot of the work in rearing him. I was more than a big brother. I was a brother, mother, and father to him. It was a great deal of responsibility to place on a ten-year-old, but living with a drunk had trained me to be more than a child even at that age.

"I took care of my brother, mother also at times, and became the hero child of the church. By high school I was leading the youth group, lay reading, ushering, and resisting the suggestions that I become a minister. I really was hearing the call from God, but I was too stubborn to respond. Had I been less stubborn my life might have been very different, and I would not carry the guilt that I live with daily.

"My father died of a cerebral hemorrhage when I was in high school. It was no surprise. Years of drinking set that in motion. It was probably a question of how, not if, drinking would kill him. My mother, brother, and I were forced onto the county relief rolls, and continued to receive help from the generosity of the congregation and its members. We felt ashamed, but we had very little choice. I became the man of the family, continued to work in the church, and steadfastly resisted God's calling.

"I was lucky that there was an opening in the county relief department after I graduated high school. They knew me there and hired me on. I went on home visits, checking the status of families and sometimes bringing them relief vouchers. After a few years, as federal programs began and there was a drive toward education, the department sent me to college to receive a social work degree. Men in social work were very rare back in those days. The professors in the program were not sure how to act toward me, but the scarcity of men gave me a great social life with the women.

"My training was rather racist. Northern cities were still exclusively white but blacks were starting to come up from the South. The northern whites didn't know what to do with them. Our social work training was from a white perspective. How do we keep the blacks from causing too much disturbance? How do we have the blacks do the menial jobs without them wanting anything more in life? I'm using the term 'black,' but back then there were other words we used that were not so nice or respectful. The fact is that whites back then did not know how to deal with blacks. They were scared and trying to cope.

"I worked for social services, worked as a volunteer in the church with the young people, watched over my mother, and dated when I could. Life was good for us, or as good for the three of us could be after being raised by an alcoholic. I slowly became more radical in my beliefs as the civil rights movement began, and I became merged with the anti-war movement.

"My little brother worked in one of the old factories that still existed then in the city but was drafted into the army. He would almost certainly be sent to Vietnam. I suggested that he escape to Canada, or enroll in college. Instead, maybe to defy me or maybe out of an unreasonable sense of patriotism, he allowed himself to be drafted and enrolled in ranger school. This would guarantee that he would be in the army several years longer than a standard draftee would have to serve.

"During the weeks before his induction we argued a great deal. I encouraged him not to go, and he insisted that it was his 'patriotic duty' to do so. Our last night ended badly. We were angry at one another as he went off to his induction. This distance hurt my mother, choosing between her two sons, and she was never quite as warm toward me as she had been before. In short, my anti-war feelings put a distance between my mother, my brother, and myself.

"Despite our anger, he continued to write to me. Never in his life had he ever called me by name and now was no exception. 'Big Brother' is always how he would address me, and his letters continued to come to 'Big Brother.' He shared with me some of the horrors that he was seeing during the war. As my anti-war activities increased, I even used his letters as evidence to support my cause. I organized rallies in the streets of the city. I recruited the younger people in the congregation to join in these rallies. As my efforts against the war increased, I became estranged from the older people, my old Sunday school teachers, and veterans of World War II. They supported the war, and I did all I could to oppose it.

"I worked during the day for the county, administrating welfare programs and doing community organization among the poor and the minorities. At night, I was organizing anti-war activities and protests at the train terminal where soldiers came home from the war and where new recruits boarded to go to boot camp. As the war continued, we got more radical. Instead of opposing the war, we began to oppose the soldiers going to war. We made signs that read 'baby killer' and 'baby killers go to hell,' and carried these at our rallies, showing them to the soldiers leaving and those arriving.

"Our church got a new minister at that time. I did a lot of political maneuvering to make sure that he was anti-war. It split the congregation, but he came. Sermons were anti-war and pro-civil rights. We no longer heard the gospel, only politics. Older members began to feel estranged and the younger ones were rude in the name of righteousness. They, as I, simply behaved badly. We did so in the name of justice and patted ourselves on the back for our righteousness. What a pride-filled creature I had become. What prideful creatures we all were.

"It was May of 1968, just a few weeks after Easter, when the final straw came. It started out as a normal protest. We held our signs and shouted 'baby killer' to the returning troops, feeling very proud of ourselves for our righteousness and knowing that we were much more Christian than the soldiers or anyone who was not opposed to the war. I walked up to one soldier who I did not recognize; a large, muscled one. I held the sign in front of him a yelled at the top of my voice, 'You are a baby killer!'

"In most cases the soldiers looked away and felt ashamed. This one flew into a rage. I could see his face distort and his eyes widen. I did not see the punch that came. I felt it. It was hard and strong. He decked me with one punch and I lay on the ground looking up at him.

"It was only then that I recognized him as my little brother.

"He looked as if he would jump on me and pound me further, but several other soldiers grabbed him and pushed him away. My fellow protestors got me to the hospital where I needed my face sutured up, and became ready to return home, not knowing what it would be like to live in the same apartment with him. I returned home and left him and my mother in the living room, as I locked myself in the bedroom.

"Neither of them were awake when I left the apartment the next morning. It was a Sunday and I was scheduled to usher. This required that I be there early. I set things up and began greeting people. People were arriving and asking what happened to my cheek. 'A soldier attacked me' was all that I would say.

"Younger worshippers congratulated me, while the older ones gave me a grimace but said nothing. The pastor congratulated me for my fine work and I felt rather pleased with myself even as I mentally condemned my brother.

"Shortly before the service started my mother and brother arrived. He had gained so much muscle weight he could not fit into his civilian clothing. Instead he wore his full-dress uniform. His old friends greeted him. Hugs and handshakes were exchanged. The pastor saw him in the narthex and walked toward him.

"'We have a policy against the war here,' the pastor explained to him. 'You may worship with us but you need to come back without your uniform. Such uniforms are not welcome here.'

"'Why should I?' my brother asked as his face grew distorted in anger. 'It is for our freedom that I have put my life at risk.'

"The pastor was quick to reply to him, 'You are a baby killer, or at least an accessory to baby killing. If you wish to return, you must do so without that satanic uniform.'

"My brother would have attacked him if it were not for my mother. She lunged in between the two men and pushed her hands against my brother's chest, pushing him back with her back to the pastor. My mother and brother left church that day, and neither ever returned, prior to their funerals.

"I continued to live in the apartment for a few weeks before moving into a shared apartment with a woman who was also an anti-war protestor. We became lovers and so I became a fornicator, even as I continued my church activities. I became estranged from my family and rarely saw them. My mother continued her sparse existence. My brother, following in my father's footsteps, became a chronic drunk, going through a series of jobs and finally becoming a recluse.

"My mother died a few years later while she slept. The coroner called it 'natural causes,' but I know that she died of a broken heart. In her will, she left everything to my baby brother. He kept up the apartment for as long as the money lasted, but finally he sold the furniture and went to live in single-room occupancy.

"I had never been against a drink but was also never a drunk. I began to become one after her death. I could not handle the guilt of her death. My drinking killed my relationship, and my girlfriend told me to move out to another apartment. And so, the life that I lived began to show consequences. I can't complain. I received the life that I deserved.

"As I drank more, my relationships at church declined. People who were supportive of me now kept me at a distance. I was drunk and isolated. It was a miracle that I kept my job. It is hard to be fired from a county job. I kept my job, but I don't know how much I really helped anyone.

"Five years after my mother died, my brother died also. He was found dead in the bathroom of his furnished room. He had stumbled and hit his head on the bathtub. He had lain there three days before he was discovered. I was his only kin. I cleaned out his personal papers and gave fifty dollars to the landlord to throw out the rest of his things. It was after I read through his personal papers that I determined that I needed to kill myself.

"He had kept a daily diary of his adventures in the army. I discovered that I was right. He really was a baby killer. Six months before he deployed home, a woman holding a bundle came running toward him. There had been incidents of suicide bombings in the area and he was taking no chances. He shot the bundle and the woman and watched her collapse on the ground. When there was no explosion he went to examine the remains. The bundle was a baby. His bullets had killed both mother and child.

"He felt legitimate pain and guilt. In his diary, he wrote that he needed to talk to his big brother, and looked forward to talking to the pastor and I. We were, for him, his way out of the dark place that he was in. I failed him, as did the minister, as did the church. We all failed him, and he died because of us.

"After reading his diary, my guilt became complete. I knew that I deserved death for causing the death of my mother and brother. I set the diary down, got very drunk, picked up one of my kitchen knives and walked to the church. It seemed appropriate that I should kill myself at the church that I had stirred up to abuse the veterans.

"A few minutes later I stood on the steps of the church, knife in hand. That was the moment that I first met Jack. He had come to pastor the church the prior year and looked out the window of the parsonage at the church steps. He saw me. Most ministers would have seen a man with a knife and called the police. Not Jack. He left the safety of his house and walked to the church step. 'Something you need to talk about?' he asked me. We started to talk and did not finish until breakfast. He convinced me to enter substance abuse rehab. This started a new relationship with him and a new life for me.

"I have been sober since then. Eventually I retired from my job at the county and entered seminary. I became ordained. Now

I serve a very small congregation, but we run a soup kitchen and serve a great deal of homeless veterans. Each week I spend a day as a volunteer at the veterans' hospital giving free counseling. This is the least I can do to repent for the harm I committed against our soldiers, my brother, and my mother.

"I deserve death, but Jack and God kept me alive so that I could repent. I now spend every day of my life trying to make up for the harm that I caused."

Harvey dropped the talking stick and burst out into tears. In a moment we surrounded him, laying our hands on him, touching him, assuring him of our presence. He cried, and we held him.

So ended the second story of our circle.

8

A Non-Mother's Pain

It took a while for Harvey to compose himself. We hugged him and let him cry. We checked the chicken in the oven and snacked on treats from the bowls. These stories were hard on the teller but just as hard on the group of supporters. At last his composure was restored and the group tasks completed. We sat once more in the circle, and Laura picked up the stick.

If I were to adopt another daughter, Laura would be the one that I would select to adopt. I adore the girl, and I have felt trauma every time I hear her story. I want to fix and heal her. Unfortunately, that is beyond my power. I can only hope that the spirit of Jesus transmitted in this group can bring her to that point.

Laura sat cross-legged on the chair with the stick on her lap, her palms up and her eyes closed. She held the pose for a few minutes before she began her story.

"I always felt God's call, but when I was young, women did not become ministers, especially in the type of church that I was raised in. I grew up in an independent fundamentalist church where I was told that to be a true Christian, a woman should become a wife, teach Sunday school, and have babies. Frankly I wouldn't have minded the baby part. I adore babies and love cuddling them, and always wanted to nurture them. I did, however, resent not being allowed to pursue what I believed God was telling me to do."

Laura paused, eyes still closed, as she worked on controlling her breathing. Her stress level was rising as she remembered and reported her hurt-filled past. We all waited; no one spoke. It was one of our firmest rules—only the one with the talking stick talks. When she was ready and able, she began again.

"I was always considered pretty, although I had few dates and few female friends. Girls were always catty with me. They were jealous of my looks. Boys enjoyed leering at me but never wanted to date me. I think I was always too tall for them and they felt insecure in my presence.

"I was rather directionless as I approached college age. I looked at various colleges, but none stood out as places that I wished to go. Instead, I chose to tour the country. I had waited tables all through high school and enjoyed a good amount of savings. With it I bought a car and headed west. I always dreamed of seeing California, and I did. My used Buick got me to Los Angeles, where I began work at a plush restaurant. It was there that a modeling scout discovered me. My career was launched.

"It was not long before my face was seen in every household in the country. I was on TV doing soap commercials and billboards advertising travel. I don't think that there was a product that I did not endorse. My family was scandalized when I began to model underwear and bikinis. I was known, I was rich, but largely dateless. Men drooled over me but were too intimidated by me to ask me out. I lived a rich but lonely life.

"All things end, of course. As I passed the mid-twenties—I know that is young for most professions, but it is old for the modeling industry—I began to get fewer of the top-paying jobs. My days were numbered, and I knew that I would need an education. While still modeling, I began my college career and was able to finish in five years with an art history degree. By now I was in my thirties with a degree but with few jobs. Frankly, I was tired of the life of modeling, California, and the celebrity life. I packed up and moved back home.

"My family was kind to me, but we were never as close as we once were. They did not appreciate how much of my skin I had presented to the world. I was able to get a hostess job while I applied for teaching positions, but I knew that I could live very comfortably from my investments. Literally to this day, I could live without working again. My only worry was that my bio-clock was ticking."

She paused waiting to regain her composure. Laura was coming to the most painful part of her story. I could hear the breathing in the quiet room as we waited. I smelled the roasting chicken and wondered if it should be checked. I restrained myself from tapping just to break that silence that was so hard for me to endure. Finally, she spoke again.

"I did a very stupid thing. I married because I wanted a family and didn't evaluate the man very well. I convinced myself that it was love but it is obvious now that it wasn't. I married a narcissist who couldn't believe that he really was marrying a former model. I was his reason to brag to his friends. It didn't give me much status, but I was looking forward to the status of motherhood. Unfortunately, that never came."

Tears flowed down her checks as she paused yet again, still sitting cross-legged on the chair, her palms still up. I wondered how any human being could possibly hold that position for so long. She controlled her breathing again and, with tears still flowing, picked up her story.

"Women called my body perfect, but it isn't. My body has a flaw. It cannot carry children. We tried but I miscarried two times in the first trimester. My husband became increasingly angry and quite abusive. I was not feeding his narcissism by bearing him sons to look like him, act like him, and carry on his name. Finally, I tried an experimental drug. It helped a bit. My last pregnancy lasted into the fifth month. This miscarriage was worse than the others. I hemorrhaged and almost bled to death. I spent three days in ICU receiving transfusions before I was declared to be out of danger. I was feeling despaired and very depressed.

"My depression deepened when my husband arrived to visit me. He told me that he was moving out and divorcing me. He wanted sons, and I could not deliver. I now knew how Anne Boleyn felt. He could not chop off my head, but he certainly took away my desire to live.

"I avoided the psych ward by not letting on to my feelings of depression and told no one of my suicidal thoughts. No one, that is, until I met Jack. He came to visit his parishioner, my hospital roommate, and we began to converse as she was sleeping. He became a mentor, a friend, and my antidote for depression. With his influence, I began to rediscover my Christian roots, but this time in a mainline tradition, not a fundamentalist setting.

"I still had my money because I had insisted on a prenuptial agreement. I enrolled in seminary. Three years later I began ministry in a small, rural parish. Being financially comfortable allowed me to work for very little money, and this thrilled the congregation. I'm still there, as a matter of fact. I settled into a nice life, knowing that I would always be barren but knowing I was finally living my calling to ministry and mothering an entire congregation. My days of depression, however, were only just beginning.

"Three years after beginning my parish work I accepted an invitation to be a volunteer chaplain at the local medical center. I volunteered twice each month. I did overnight shifts which lasted fifteen hours.

"When I began I most feared the accidents and traumas that I would see in the emergency department. This hospital was the major trauma center, and so accidents and severe injuries were common. I feared these, but I found them to be manageable. I sat in support and prayer with dozens of accident patients and the families of the survivors and the deceased. As hard and taxing as the work was, I enjoyed it. In the parish, there is not a lot of instant gratification. Being a chaplain for the severely injured brings immediate results. I was doing good work in a way that was satisfying and was happy to be doing it until I hit a wall—a hard wall that weighed less than three pounds.

"We carried beepers so that we might be summoned for emergencies. I was beeped to the neonatal intensive care unit, NICU. A woman had delivered prematurely, and she was not certain that the child would survive. She asked for an emergency baptism.

"It was on the way to the unit when I could almost feel the birth pangs that I had three times endured, only to have deceased babies. My muscles began to spasm and my limbs began to shake. Somehow, I summoned the strength to walk out of the elevator. The nurse who had summoned me greeted me there.

"'Thank you for coming, Chaplain,' she said. 'A mom, Mary Murphy, needs you. She wants a baptism.'

"'Will the child live?' I asked.

"'We don't know.'

"My heart began to race, and my head began to throb. I carefully placed one foot in front of the other as I slowly followed the nurse into NICU nursery number 3. We walked past the incubators of four babies before coming to a crying woman sitting vigil next to one of the many incubators. Mary Murphy looked like her name, with her curly red hair, slight frame, and sparkling green eyes. I strode to her as the nurse introduced us.

"'Mary, you want a baptism, is that correct?'

"'Yes. If my boy dies I want him in heaven with his grandmother.'

"'I can certainly do that for you. Do you have any faith background?'

"'Yes,' she said, looking embarrassed. 'I grew up Lutheran but have not really been active in years. Is that a problem?'

"'No, Mary. I will do this for you and your boy.'

"I looked at him. He was tiny even by NICU standards, and I knew that his chances of survival were slim. In a flashback, I could see my own little boy whom I had miscarried and who had never taken so much as one breath. He had been my first. A little girl had been my second. The third was also a boy, though I had never seen him; I had been unconscious from my own blood loss. I fought to keep my mind in the present, as the thought of my boy became intrusive.

"'Are you all right, Laura?' Mary asked.

"'Yes, fine. Just sad for you.' I knew that I needed to get out of this situation as quickly as possible.

"'What is his name?'

"'Brian James Murphy.'

"'I picked up the bottle of sterile water from the bedside. My stomach was churning as I opened it, dipped my fingers into it, and pushed my hand through the opening in the side of the heated crib.' Brian James Murphy, I baptize you in the name of the Father, Son, and the Holy Spirit. O Lord, we pray your healing hand upon this your child. Heal him body, mind, and spirit. Bless your servant Mary as she cares for this child, a gift from you. Bless the staff that cares for the babies and the families. Give them loving hearts, strong arms, and wise minds that your children may grow to be healthy, blessed, and faithful to you. I pray in Jesus' name. Amen.'"

"'Amen,' Mary repeated. 'Thank you for doing this.'

"'You are very welcome. Is there anything else that I can do for you?'

"'No, just keep saying prayers for me and my boy.'

"My stomach, which had been churning since the prayer began, now felt like it would explode. I walked quickly out of the nursery and toward the bathroom. My mind flashed back to the memories of the three babies that my body had rejected. None had been baptized. Stillborn children were not baptized.

"I entered the bathroom only seconds before my stomach rejected its contents. My stomach muscles ached from the assault my body was waging against me. I don't know how long it lasted but my knees became sore from kneeling on the hard tiles. I hoped I was finished as the emergency beeper again wailed. I checked the number and I felt sad and anxious when I saw the code for the maternity ward.

"I cleaned myself up and rinsed my mouth before taking the stairs down two flights and swiping my badge into the unit. Patty, a tiny Irish nurse, who had the heart of an angel, with whom I had worked before, met me by the station.

"'Thanks for coming,' she said. 'There is an angry woman who had a stillborn child. She hasn't asked to see anyone, but I think she can use your presence.'

"'I'll check on her, Patty.'

"I entered the room and saw a large woman with an angry face. She sat five feet away from the bassinet that held her deceased child wrapped in a blanket.

"'Who are you?' she demanded.

"'I'm the chaplain. The nurse called me. She said that you had lost a child.'

"'I don't want to talk to anyone. Why don't you just get yourself out of here?'

"'It is hard to lose a child. I've done that. I'm here for you if you need.'

"'I don't care about your troubles, lady. I didn't want this kid. It was my boyfriend's idea. You can take that dead thing, throw it out, and get yourself out of here.'

"I felt something rise in me. It was disbelief. It was a rage. An old memory, long forgotten, flooded into me. Her telling me that the pregnancy was not her idea triggered me in a way that I wouldn't have predicted. I flashed back to a time when I was a little girl. I fought to control the memory that was becoming more intrusive.

"'You don't even want a blessing for your baby?' I asked her.

"'If you don't shut up and get yourself out of here, they'll be calling security to take me off of you. Understand?'

"She attempted to rise but was slow, so I was never in danger. I let myself out, and was grateful not to see Patty. What I really needed was another bathroom.

"I found one outside the unit and my stomach emptied itself again. The intrusive thoughts came back to me. I saw my mother lying in a blood-covered bed, a stillborn fetus next to her. She was unconscious. I was the reason that she lived but I was also the reason that she was close to death. I saved her life by calling for an ambulance. But I had jeopardized her life by convincing her to have this pregnancy.

"I had an older brother but longed for a sister. I had begged and pleaded with my mother to give me a sister. She and my father were hesitant. Her two pregnancies were difficult and there were the financial factors. I guess I was persuasive. My parents worked on giving me a little sister, and my mother's figure ballooned as the little one took life. It ended after five months, with the miscarriage and my mother's near-death experience.

"The memory, now released, overwhelmed my soul with guilt. I cried over the toilet as I remembered the pain that I caused my own mother. I was guilty of not honoring her.

"When finally, I regained my self-control, I left the bathroom. It was almost seven o'clock. My shift did not end for an hour. I made my way to the office to write out my overnight report. I found a note from my supervisor informing me that he was in the building but at another meeting. He was not able to debrief my night. I waited until eight, left my report on the desk, put my beeper into the charger, and walked to my car.

"I had a blackout as one would from a drinking binge, except I hadn't been drinking. I sat in my car and looked at my watch. It told me that it was ten o'clock. What had happened over the last two hours? I had never had a blackout before, and it frightened me. I felt enraged by the woman in maternity, guilty by the memories flashing back, and now scared by the blackout. I needed to be home.

"I drove the standard route to my house, which passed a Planned Parenthood clinic. Usually I drove by at eight in the morning, not ten. I was accustomed to seeing it closed. Today there was a line of pregnant women ready to enter. My anger boiled like a volcanic rage. How could women be getting abortions? Didn't they know how hard it is to lose a child? I parked the car ready to cross the street and confront them. The only thing that stopped me was my phone ringing. It was Jack, calling me to have me join one of his committees.

"He heard the guilt, rage, and depression in my voice. Soon he was there picking me up and taking me out for coffee. I spent months in therapy and took an antidepressant. I wasn't much good to anyone for a while. Jack visited with me once a week until I was recovered.

"Since then I have added another volunteer activity to my week. I started a mother's relief group. I have recruited volunteers who go to visit new mothers. We give mothers a two-hour break each day. We don't want them ever to view their children as a burden. Those who register with us get up to ten hours free each week. That is their time to use as they please. It is Momma's respite."

Laura put the stick down and burst out in tears. We surrounded her, holding her, letting her feel the warmth of humans who loved and cared for her. Finally, her tears ended, but we continued to hold her.

9

Silent Supper

aura left her chair and ran toward me. I stood to embrace her. The others, except for Will, circled around holding her. Will, looking overwhelmed by the group and the stories, hung back, still trying to take all this in. I hugged Laura and let her cry, even as I looked at Will and wondered if I had made a mistake in having him join the group. Was it too much for him?

"I need to eat," Laura said as she began to pull away. "I need food."

It was time to eat. The food smelled like it was finished and we were halfway through our circle of stories. One at a time, we walked toward the kitchen.

"Will," I said, "we have assigned seating here. It goes in the order of joining the circle. Harvey will be at the end of the table; you sit on his right, across from me. Except for the grace that we will say before the meal, we eat in silence until the next storyteller begins."

Will looked at me and nodded slowly. He had the look of being overwhelmed with the day and I could not blame him. He had heard many stories for the first time, each painful. It was a great deal for anyone to take in.

I stood by my place at the table; Laura would soon be sitting to my left. Walter would be sitting at the far end when he was done putting food on the table. Across the table near Walter would be Madeline; between her and Will, Ralph would sit. Ralph and Walter had long ago established the tradition of cooking and serving. They seemed to enjoy it more than most of us.

The platters and dishes were standard commercial china with black rings around the circumference. They had been donated from kitchens of closed churches through the classis or in some cases they were from churches upgrading their china and disposing of the old. Soon we would be looking at these old used plates full of new food: chicken, roasted potatoes, and green beans, all set out on the long, thick wooden table.

Laura rushed around the table with a water pitcher, filling glasses. She was full of nervous energy, unable to speak or contain her emotions. Finally, the glasses were filled, and the platters and bowls set in the center. We all sat down and joined hands.

"Oh God," I spoke softly. All in the room repeated back to me. It was our custom—antiphonal prayer.

"Thank you for this wonderful food."

I waited for the response.

"Thank you for those buying it and preparing it."

Again, I waited for the others to respond, feeling a bit self-serving as I had purchased the food.

"Nurture us with it as you nurture us with your Spirit."

They responded softly, contemplatively.

"Through Jesus we pray. Amen."

They finished and I sat receiving platters, taking food, and passing platters. I inhaled deeply, celebrating the wonderful smells, coping with the quiet as best I could. Silverware clinked against plates. The sounds of chewing and swallowing interrupted the uncomfortable silence. I ate my food slowly, studying the faces and feeling the emotions.

Will, across from me, looked down at his plate, refusing to make eye contact. He ate little and continued to look stunned. Between he and I sat Harvey at the end of the table. He never lost his appetite at any of these gatherings. His substantial belly gave testimony to his ability to eat despite the circumstances.

Laura sat next to me ritualizing her meal. She would place a forkful of food into her mouth, set down the utensil, and chew her food slowly. Only after each mouthful was chewed and swallowed did she pick up her fork and begin her next mouthful.

Walter ate ravenously no matter where he was, under any circumstances. So it was that he sat quietly, staring off across the table as if he was looking at something that no one else could see. His hands moved rapidly as he ate. Somehow he found his food with his fork, even though his eyes never went toward the plate. Perhaps he was remembering his story that he would be sharing shortly.

Madeline ate little. She gave the appearance of being traumatized. She was recalling her own demons. She ate little, as was normal and expected. Her petite body never seemed to require much food despite her high-energy level and her constant movement. She sat now twirling her dark hair with her left hand, even as she pushed her food around with the fork. She looked more troubled than the others.

Between Madeline and Will sat Ralph, the youngest of our group. Tall with blonde hair, he looked barely out of school. He had eaten quickly and now sat staring at his empty plate with a hand on each cheek. With these he supported his head, his eyes seemingly ready to tear.

I listened to the quiet meal, grateful for the small noises of clattering silverware and the swallows of the wounded.

10

Evicted Children

The silence finally ended as Walter pushed away his plate, drank down the last of his water, and set his glass next to his plate. He then turned to the sideboard behind him to retrieve the talking stick. There was silence in the room as he held it in both hands and stared at it. His eyes glazed, as his mind dredged up his own painful memory. We all sat in silence until he began to speak.

"I was one of the few Cubans who was not raised Catholic. It is a long story how my family came to be Protestant, much less Reformed Protestant, but we were raised in that faith. My parents were born and raised in New York City, got college educations, and moved to New Jersey. They wanted my sister and I to have a safer neighborhood to be raised in. We settled into the New Jersey suburbs, attended a Reformed church, and lived the American dream.

"My parents were thrilled when I went to a Reformed college and then a Reformed seminary, but they divorced toward the end of my first year. My father was never the nicest man to live with, but my mother had stayed with him for the sake of us children. After I left for school, he had an affair; and with me gone there was nothing to keep them together. I remained close to my mother and was a Latino mom's dream—faithful, religious and even ordained!

"I am not sure quite what group I fell in with at seminary. I felt uncomfortable with the fundamentalists. The other Latinos thought I should be part of the charismatic movement. In reality I was more of a mainstream Reformed that harkened back to past generations. I guess one might have defined me as 'middle of the road,' and I let no one else define me or pull me into their camps. That was always my blessing and that was always my curse. I could steer my own ship despite obstacles, but not always did I listen to advice.

"One thing that I was in those early days of ministry was prideful. I was not aware of it at the time, but I was as proud as any Pharisee that Jesus condemned. I just knew that I had the ability to transform any life, grow any church, and make people reevaluate their lives from an encounter with me. I guess I saw myself as a Jedi knight who, with the wave of a hand, could change hearts and minds."

Walter held the stick but faced his head down to look at the table. He looked pained and filled with shame. Every muscle in his body seemed to tense with anger and self-loathing. I could see Will wanting to rise and comfort him. His nurturing instincts were coming back to life as he was coming out of himself, but the timing of his nurturing was not right. Each person needed to tell his or her story. I motioned to Will to stay seated. Harvey gently reached his arm out, tapped his forearm, and gestured to him that all would be all right. Will sat back in his chair, pensively following our directions.

It was a long few minutes before Walter began again.

"Several years after starting to pastor my second congregation, a crisis began. A new live-in janitor was hired.

He and his family moved into the apartment on premises. The family, composed of new immigrants to the country, were excited for this opportunity. It was the best living circumstances that they had ever seen. The family was thrilled to move in and hoped to become part of us.

"Not everyone was excited that they had arrived. Some of the congregation did not want us to hire immigrants. When I reminded them that my grandparents were immigrants, they seemed to think that the second generation was somehow legitimized compared to immigrants or the first generation. I was asked if I 'couldn't find an American' to fill this job.

"There were others who did not like this family because of a more selfish reason: These people had not been appointed to the search committee. The consistory had appointed one committee to make the hire, which was the committee that I worked with. These two church members were put out from the start, because they were not 'consulted' in the process. I tried to soothe them as best I could, but they would not be soothed. Their ongoing criticism was constant and cruel. The family was never fully able to become part of our community. They sat on the side of our fellowship, estranged and criticized.

"I attempted to bridge the chasm that stood between the group and this family. We all lived on the church property and I attempted to be a mentor for the family children, especially the boy. He let me get close, but not too close. There was always a wall that he put up when he felt the need. He seemed to fear closeness. Something was wrong. I assumed that since church members kept him at bay he didn't quite trust me either."

Walter paused once more. The storytelling was stressful on all of us but for him it wasn't recalling it, he was reliving it with all the trauma that he felt when first he had experienced it. He rolled the stick back and forth between his two palms for several moments. The rhythm and the touch seem to ground him and give him strength, so that he was able to continue.

"A crisis began when money started to be missing from one of our closets. This closet held the Sunday collections until they could be counted on Monday. Mission baskets often stayed there for weeks until a mission drive was concluded. Our counters noticed that small amounts would be missing from the mission baskets—three dollars here, a ten-dollar bill gone another day. The old guard of the church, who managed the money, were convinced that it was the janitor. I asked how they knew and they could not give me an answer, but they distrusted the family and gave them the blame. They demanded a firing. I wanted to be certain.

"With the help of two church members I organized a stakeout. The accusations were confirmed. The janitor's son was using a key, entering the closet, and taking cash, all while the youth choir practiced on Sunday afternoon. He was confronted, and his father was called. He admitted the thefts and explained that he did it for extra spending money. The question now became what to do next.

"Consistory agreed that I should begin meeting weekly with the boy. Our old guard was angry that we had not had him arrested, or at least evicted the family from our premises. I must have heard a dozen times 'We told you,' from those who had opposed the family. They bristled at the consistory's decision and the criticism increased. I met with the boy regularly but wondered if I made any progress. Again, he seemed to let me get so close but never truly trusted me.

"I suspected that the boy was keeping a big family secret, and frequently visited the family in addition to the boy. They lived like slobs. I wondered if I was simply projecting my own family values on them. I was convinced that I could transform the boy as well as the rest of the family. It was my pride at work. I could not conceive that with enough effort I would not make positive changes within the family and be a catalyst to reconcile the family and the church.

"For six months, there was a détente between the congregation at large and the family. I did not hear constant cries for firing and eviction, but there was constant criticism of the work that was done. They failed to remember that the old guard members had hounded out the two prior janitors in the very same way. Clearly no janitor would ever work long or hard enough to satisfy this group.

"After six months, the somewhat peaceful arrangement ended. A counselling center in our building began reporting money missing. The therapist who worked the center kept careful daily record of income but each day there were small amounts missing. The pattern seemed to be the same as the last series of robberies, except these had to be occurring overnight. Would a high school student really be staying up overnight to carry out robberies?

"I did another stake-out—this time overnight—and I was joined by a church member who was a retired police officer. We found our culprit, it was the janitor. It was in my office while waiting for the police that he told me about the thefts. He was a heroin addict and was stealing to support his drug use. I watched in sadness and shame as he was taken out in handcuffs, but the worst was yet to come.

"It was now five in the morning. I needed to be in criminal court at ten. Sleep-deprived or not, I needed to be present for the arraignment. I went home, showered, cooked breakfast for my children, and then told them the bad news. They, of course, had played many hours with the janitor's children. Mine were younger by a few years but they had still played together. After breakfast and before the drive to school, I told them that their friend's father had been arrested and that I had caused this incarceration."

Walter grew silent and stared at the table. At first his eyes glistened and soon afterward a few small tears began their journey down his cheeks before dripping onto the table. He rotated the stick once again, but this time faster. It was almost a frenzy that he had worked himself into as he sublimated his negative energy into the stick. We waited. Each of us had different levels of patience for waiting, but no one was as uncomfortable with silence as me. Finally, my agony ended as I heard Walter's voice begin again.

"The morning was hard to endure as I waited for him to be brought before the judge in handcuffs. I was angry that he had betrayed my trust in him, and humbled that my efforts had not brought a better end to my family intervention. I also dreaded the comments and reaction from my dissenters in the congregation and the emergency consistory meeting that was to follow.

"Ultimately he struck a plea bargain and entered drug rehabilitation, after he cooperated in naming the local drug dealers. In the wake of his cooperation several raids and arrests were made. The consistory insisted on firing and eviction. The next day I delivered the news in person and by letter to the mother, informing her that she and her children would be moving. I collected the church keys and almost cried when the youngest daughter looked into my eyes, told me how much she loved this house in a safe neighborhood, and asked why she had to move even though she had done nothing wrong.

"My detractors insisted that I evict the family immediately. I waited until the family had found new housing. It seemed easy for those against me to call for an immediate eviction when they were not the ones who were throwing children out of their home. I viewed them as 'armchair quarterbacks' and endured their comments and criticisms.

"It took months, but they finally did leave for a new house. As they packed to move, the younger daughter simply stared at me with sad and angry eyes. It nearly broke my heart. Guilt surged within me as I walked into self-doubt, wondering if there had been anything I could have done to create a different outcome.

"I tried to stay in touch with this family, but they never responded. I saw the son several years later. He was in the rookie year of what he thought was the beginning of a career in the police department. I was visiting a patient at the local hospital when he and his police partner were bringing in an arrested man for treatment. The man was the suspect in a bar fight. We chatted for a few minutes, but he didn't seem happy to speak with me. I felt happy that he seemed to have gone 'straight' after his experiments with burglary.

"My happiness at his straightening his life out was rather short-lived. Not long after seeing him I read in the local newspaper that he was suspended. It was alleged that he had assaulted a handcuffed prisoner that he had in custody. He was fired from the department, and his certification as a police officer in the state was taken from him.

"Several years later the father was also in the newspaper. He had been fired from his second job as a cook shortly after his arrest. Eventually he settled into a job as a bus driver for special-needs children. I was shocked that a bus company would allow a man with such a history to have such a job with children. Nevertheless, he was hired. The newspaper report I read spoke of his firing and arrest, on accusations that he had assaulted an autistic child with a stick. His excuse was that the student annoyed him with the noises he was making and he was seeking to quiet the child who would not obey his verbal commands for silence. I never did hear the outcome of that arrest.

"For months after the eviction I walked in a daze, not quite feeling anything. I was almost numb. I had troubled focusing on my work, and the little girl and her sad, angry eyes haunted me in my dreams. I guess I was depressed, although no one ever diagnosed me as such. Pastoring became difficult, as my focus was diminished and I heard the constant words of the critics who second-guessed my decision to hire the janitor at all. I doubted myself.

"Jack, during one of our regional meetings, approached me. He had sensed or observed that I was not myself. I don't know what it was that alerted him to my state but I am happy that he figured it out. He sat me down and told me that I looked troubled. I tried to deny it. I guess I was ashamed of being so depressed. He simply looked at me, smiled and told me to stop lying to him. He then told me that he and I would be talking after the meeting. He said it in a way that made it clear that this was not a request. It was an instruction.

"We talked for several hours that evening and weekly for two months after that. Jack brought me to one of his circle meetings and I have been here since. I still am haunted by the sadness of the little girl's face but I found a way to make things right in my mind.

"I gathered some Spanish-speaking Christians in our town and organized a group to protect the rights of the migrant laborers. We bring lunches to those who have not gotten work and translate between them and those who hire them so that they are treated fairly. We find out what employers do not treat people well and warn other laborers. We learn who does bad work and counsel them to do better work.

"Every so often the workers show me pictures of their children that their work supports and they thank me for helping them support their families. Each smiling face I see from those pictures helps expunge the image of the sad, evicted girl. And so, I live my life to take away the pain of that memory."

Walter set the stick down, held his head in his hands and grew very quiet. He did not sob, as it was not his nature. Instead we all sobbed for him before we surrounded him, held him, and assured him of our presence with him.

11

Abducted

It took awhile, but we helped Walter find his composure. He passed the stick to Madeline, as we scurried to sit down once again. Of all the stories that were shared in this group, hers was the one that bothered me most. Whenever she told it I found my body tensing and a rage building. She was petite and came from a pure French heritage. She looked like a little girl, and my protective instincts rose when I listened to her recollect her story. Now I waited, ready to hear her story that always caused feelings of rage within me. She took the stick and set it before her.

"All four of my grandparents were immigrants to this country from France following the war. My parents, while living here, had pride and arrogance taught them by their parents. My father was a banker and my mother a nurse. They were not always nice. My father was crude and angry; my mother was under his control and dispersed her anger onto her children. She was always critical of us and our achievements and never nurturing. She treated us horribly, although it was a bit more subtle.

"As a nurse she was aware of every threat to our safety. She was afraid. We were different from other children in the area. Often we were not allowed to play outside. My mother would claim that it was 'too damp.' Water fights in the summers amused other parents. To my mother they were cause for concern. We would 'get sick and die.'

"We were taught that we were better than others. We French were more cultured and Americans, crude. My sister believed these things that we were told. To this day she is arrogant but suffers from substance-abuse issues and an eating disorder. She has nothing in her career to be proud of but still looks down on others.

"With my family being French we were educated, of course, in Catholic schools. What else was there? It was not always an easy fit for me. I was pious and faithful but the nuns and priests were not ready to have pious young people ask questions. They expected the pious to be reciting prayers and repeating verbatim what we had been taught to say. I could never understand how the church that was shaped by Aquinas should be so averse to questions and creative thinking. I spent many hours sitting in detention, contemplating my 'pride.'

"I matured physically very young and received a great deal of attention from the boys. Although our school was segregated by gender there was a boys' school across the street. It was our 'brother school' and we had dances together. I got more attention than the other girls, and that instilled a bit of jealousy in them.

"The nuns also looked at me with more suspicion now that I had matured. They had already looked down on me for asking questions. Now they looked at me as if I was doing wrong for being prettier and more developed than my classmates. I was devout, more devout than most of my peers, but I felt estranged from that community.

"Gradually my social life declined except for a very few friends. I devoted myself to my studies. I engaged in biblical studies, theology, and devotional studies. I began to question why the church I loved had such contradictory views of sex. It was godly to be celibate and it was godly to risk your life having too many pregnancies, but having two children and taking birth-control pills was a mortal sin. Was this celebrating Jesus as we were supposed to do?

"Of course I went to a Catholic college. It was the first time in my life that I was away from home. I was looking forward to being away from the chaos of my parents. My sister went to school close to home. She returned home each weekend. I was looking to be away while she was comfortable being close and safe.

"It was in college that I began to realize that I was different, in another way, from most people I knew. I had fewer memories of my childhood than most people had. The other girls in the dorm spoke endlessly about their birthday-party memories and vacation trips with their families. I had relatively few memories. Certainly my childhood was not a blank, but I came to realize that certain periods of my life had left very few memories. I assumed it was all the studying that I did had made me more aware of my books and less aware of my surroundings. I thought little of it.

"College was good to me. I was away from the controlling chaos of my family and I met a professor who was a wonderful mentor to me. He told me that my thinking was similar to that of Protestant thinkers. He encouraged me to read Luther, Calvin, and Wesley. Wesley I had no time for and quickly gave up on him. Luther I enjoyed, but I was much more drawn to Calvin. I made his *Institutes* my main study aside from my regular classes. With him I began to find what I had been seeking.

"The next step in my faith journey was seeking Reformed churches. They were many in my area of Northern New Jersey and I visited them one after another. Two of the blessings from these visits were meeting Jack for the first time, as he did summer preaching. While speaking with him, he introduced me to the Heidelberg Catechism. When I first found it and read it through, I knew that I had found the home for my faith. I kept in touch with Jack, and he helped me understand it more fully. He also came to be my unofficial spiritual guide.

"I spent my junior year of college attending a Reformed church in my area. I felt affirmed there but increasingly estranged in my Catholic college. My peers could not understand why one would attend a non-Catholic church but their faithfulness and piety were somewhat lacking. It was a dichotomy I could not quite understand. How could one not attend church but question another for attending a different church?

"Through the encouragement of the pastor where I attended church I began to consider becoming clergy, something I could not have imagined in the Catholic tradition. I joined the Reformed Church and applied to New Brunswick Seminary. This good French Catholic girl who was fluent in French earned an English degree from a Catholic college, joined a Reformed church and enrolled in a Reformed seminary. Was this a true example of God's providence, or was I simply confused?

"My years of New Brunswick were wonderful. I finally felt as if I had found a place reserved for me in the world. I thrived in this environment, graduated, and because I had taken training in clinical pastoral education I was eligible for a CPE residency. I was considering having chaplaincy as my full-time calling. This full-time residency would enable me to discern this."

Her face changed as she paused her story. All of what she had said so far was background. Her true story had yet to be told. I knew the trauma of what was coming and I, like the rest of the group, waited patiently. Her eyes seemed to drift away to another time and place. She was leaving the safety of Calvin House and entering the place of her trauma. She was not going to tell her story—she would be reliving it.

"It was an evening in April, the Thursday before Palm Sunday. I was doing the overnight shift of the hospital and had settled into bed of the chaplain's on-call room. It was after midnight when the beeper signaled a call to me. The display told me to call the emergency department. I called, quickly dressed myself, and started toward the unit where the charge nurse would be briefing me. I was feeling anxious. Nothing good ever comes from a late-night summons to an emergency department.

"The nurse told me that the patient was a sexual assault victim who was blaming herself for the attack and wished a chaplain to hear her 'confess' so that God would not be punishing her anymore. Since she was asking for confession I assumed that she must be Catholic. That type of thinking reminded me a great deal of my Catholic childhood.

"The supervising nurse escorted me into the trauma room. I observed a young woman laying on the bed sobbing, and a uniformed policewoman sitting guard inside the room. The nurse explained who I was to the police officer and swore her to confidentiality. I walked to the bed, pulled over a chair, and sat next to the patient.

"'I'm Madeline,' I said. 'I'm a chaplain here. I'm here to help you any way I can. What is it that you need from me?'

"'I need to do an act of contrition so God doesn't do anything else to me,' the young girl said to me.

"My heart jumped as she said this. All of the guilt from my Catholic background came flooding up to the surface. I fought to push these negative feelings down. I needed to be here and present for this girl.

"'Might I ask your name?'

"'I'm Mary Kate. Let me tell you what happened, and you tell me what penance I need to do to make my guilt go away.'

"I wanted so much to shake her and tell her that she was not guilty. She was the victim here, but she was blaming herself. What good would it have done?

"'Since my first communion I have promised to serve Jesus well. I have tried to be faithful. This week I failed, and God has showed me his wrath. I am a student at the Catholic college across town. I am studying there and have considered entering a convent,' she told me.

"She then stopped, grabbed my hand, and squeezed it as she began to sob. She had a very small frame and did not look strong, but her grip was uncomfortable. Perhaps adrenalin was flowing through her. I noticed a rather ugly gauze bandage on her wrist.

"'I was slothful in my devotion this week. At the beginning of Lent, I promised God that I would not miss Mass even one week. Last Sunday I broke my promise. I overslept and missed the Mass on campus. Oversleeping was a sin, but the beers that I drank the night before were even more sinful. They made me oversleep and when I woke I had a wicked headache. I simply could not make myself move.

"'Still, there was a chance for me to keep my promise to God. There was an evening Mass at a church near the campus. It was only a few blocks from my dorm and an easy walk. My promise could still be kept. I ate dinner early to give myself enough time only to allow myself to be distracted. Six of us had dinner together. We all were teasing a friend of ours about her new boyfriend. We enjoyed laughter as the time ticked by. I was horrified when I looked at the large clock in the cafeteria and noticed that the Mass would now be ending. I had broken my Lenten promise.'

"Her grip, which had relaxed now began to tighten again. She paused, and tears flowed as she sobbed. I waited until she was ready to continue.

"'I said five Hail Marys before I went to bed, and knew that such a small penance would never be enough. How can one get mercy from such a halfhearted gesture? God punished me tonight.'

"Again she paused, and I could feel my adrenaline rise. I was angry at her for blaming herself. I was angry at a church that could so forget God's mercy and instill such guilt. I wanted to speak, but knew that the only godly thing that I could do was to be present and listen.

"'I went to study at Rusty's,' she continued, 'one of the favorite hangouts for students from my college. I finished my work and was returning when I noticed the man next to his van. He wore a wool ski mask. I didn't think anything of it. It was cold for this time of year and we had a small coating of snow. He asked me what time it was, and I took my eyes off him as I reached to move my sleeve and glove to view my watch. In that moment he grabbed me, put a knife to my neck, and forced me into the back of the van.'

"Part of doing a good act of contrition is to be telling the whole story so that a proper penance can be assigned. Despite myself, I waited.

"'In the van he quickly threw me on my belly and bound my wrists with binder's twine. He told me that if I wanted to live, I would obey him and do as he wished. Next, he took duct tape from his bag and wrapped it around my head and mouth. Finally, he tied my ankles tightly with the twine. Once satisfied that I could do nothing, he climbed to the front of the van and we began driving.

"'How long did we drive? I do not know. The police asked me this many times. I'm not certain. I'm guessing for twenty or maybe thirty minutes.

"'Finally, we stopped. He left the driver's seat and approached me. He asked if I remembered the rules. I could only nod in reply; I wished to live. He took a box cutter from his bag and began slicing my clothes from me. I was left naked lying in front of him on the cold floor of the van.'

"Her body shuddered as she remembered the coldness of the man and the temperature of the van. Her tight grip held me as her body shook.

"'He pulled his pants down. I turned away. Enraged, he pulled my hair and slapped me several times before ordering me to look at him. I did not have to look long. I would have screamed but there was too much tape, and it was on too tight. Maybe it saved my life but I don't know.'

"I identified too much with her because of my own background. I felt my mind leaving my body and drifting back into my memories.

"'He turned me over and threw me back on the floor of the van and I thought he was finished with me. After pulling my hair to make me sit up he brandished his box cutter. He reminded me of his rule to do as I was told.'

"I fought the nausea from hearing her description," Madeline continued. "I disassociated once more as a new memory flooded me, one of my childhood friend, Angela. I walked into her alley to find her only to see her landlord abusing her. My presence ended the encounter but she always looked ashamed now that I knew of her abuse. She had told me to tell no one and I didn't. I've always wondered if I should have. Now I was with a good Catholic girl and I was identifying too much with her experience. How could I be of help to her?

"'He now pulled my legs up, cut the cords of my ankles, and pulled them apart. He knew that I was a virgin and he taunted me for that. I felt guilty.' Her crying became worse. I held her hand, fighting my own demons and being disgusted that she could have been treated in such a way and that she could blame herself. The nurse opened the door to check on Mary Kate as the sounds of her anguish were heard outside of the room. It was a while before she could continue.

"'Finally, this torture would end. I hoped to die but wished to see my parents one more time. I prayed for an angel to kill this man, but none came. Finally, he threw my legs down and once more pulled me up by my hair. He told me that if I cooperated with the police he would come again to me and give me a mastectomy. He held up my driver's license from my wallet and told me he could find me. To prove that he meant this, he sliced my breast with his cutter.'

"She let go of my hand, pulled her gown up, and showed me her breast. I saw a long wound neatly stitched.

"'You see what he did to me? It took thirty-seven stitches to close that. Thirty-seven.'

"She sobbed more, and trembled violently. Even the policewoman seemed agitated. She repeatedly shifted in her seat and rubbed the butt of her sidearm. I have no doubt what she would have done had she met the man who did this to Mary Kate.

"'He tied my ankles once more, gagged me once again, and began to drive. Again, I don't know how long the drive was. My body hurt too much to care.

"'At last, the van stopped. He came to the back, opened the rear door, and rolled me out. I was tied, naked, and gagged in the street. I broke my shoulder in the fall. Slowly he drove away, and I wondered if I would die from the next car that would come.

"'I didn't. A driver saw me, stopped the car, and called the police. He put a blanket over me, and for the first time all evening I received a bit of compassion. They tell me that this was midnight and I left the diner at nine. All of this took three hours.

"'You are not a priest but you are religious. I need a penance. Give me one that God will not send another attack. Pray for me that I am not pregnant. I cannot bring his child into this world, but I cannot have an abortion. That, you know, would be a mortal sin.'

"I was crying with her as I sought to repress again my memories that she had stirred up. I, like she, fought nausea and I even felt chilled. My job was to be there for her, but I was struggling to do so. I paused, my mind racing. Finally, I spoke.

"'You must,' I told her, 'say three hail Marys, to remind yourself that other women have suffered greatly. You must say three Our Fathers to remind yourself that God has not abandoned you but wants the best for you. You must go to the rape crisis center for weekly counseling until they tell you that you no longer need it. Then your sins will be forgiven, and you will find healing.'

"There was a pause as she thought of these things. She then kissed my hand and thanked me, before returning to her sobs and shaking. She said nothing more. I continued to hold her hand until she fell asleep. Shortly after that she was moved to her room, the police guard accompanying her. At last she was sleeping but I could not.

"I was off the next two days. On the third day I went to see her, but she had been discharged. I never saw her again. Regulations precluded us from contacting patients once they were no longer patients. I was deprived of my chance to check on her.

"She haunted me in my dreams. I woke frequently and became sleep-deprived. My chaplain supervisor was no help. He told me that I would get over it in time; he failed as a trauma counselor. I was left to myself, to my dreams and to her sobbing. I finished my residency but was mostly going through motions. I doubt that I was much help to anyone. My wounds were too deep and too exposed. Finally, I thought of Jack. I don't know why I did. Perhaps God was telling me to. I called him and he met me.

"When I told him my story he picked me up as Mary held Jesus in the Pieta. 'Cry,' he commanded, 'cry.' As Mary cried for Jesus, as Mary Kate cried, so I cried in his arms and my journey toward healing had begun."

12

Millstones for The Neck

It seemed like hours, but in reality it was only minutes before Madeline composed herself and passed the stick to Ralph. The baton had been passed from the shortest to the tallest member of our group. Ralph, a fourth-generation Dutchman, was taller than I and had broader shoulders; his light blonde hair and clear blue eyes rounded out the picture.

"I grew up in a small Reformed church in a largely Catholic area. We were a distinct minority. I didn't mind it so much, but I always felt different from others my age in my area. Often, I went to Catholic Youth Organization events. My parents were third-generation Dutch and had lived in the Dutch enclave where they had grown up, before a job transfer brought my family into a more urban and non-Dutch Reformed area. The church I was raised in was nothing special or remarkable, but it was warm and loving.

"I walked in two different worlds, that of my church culture and that of a largely secular city with Catholic identity. I was a bit jealous of my Dutch relatives who still lived in the Protestant-dominated world of the Midwest, where people had heard of and respected the Reformed Church. In my neighborhood, people would ask me what a Protestant was and ask what the Reformed

Church was reformed from. When I was young I really didn't know, and had no answer to give.

"There was one place in my part of the world, besides my church, where I felt that I really belonged, and that was summer camp. It was a mainline Protestant camp that served young peopie in eastern Pennsylvania and western New Jersey. My parents sent me there each summer for a week, or two if I was lucky. There I could relate to everyone. They knew church and Protestant traditions. These were my people, and I was theirs.

"These summers at the seemingly endless rolling hills and woods of the camp became my image of heaven. We swam, boated, sang, hiked, and worshipped. The counselors were the most loving people that I had ever met. More than loving, they were cool. They were the people that I wanted to be. I idolized the camp staff. Perhaps I committed a sin by idolizing them. I paid quite a price for that mistake."

I watched Ralph as he paused. He stared at the table, not daring to look any of us in the eye. He was tapping into his guilt—or maybe it was shame, which was perhaps the most sinister and destructive of all human feelings. There was a very long pause, much longer than the others had exhibited, as he readied himself to return to his story. Tears streamed down his face as he began. His voice was hard to understand, and his throat tightened with his memories.

"When I was young I was an in-camper. In high school I did out-camping," he continued. "I did backpacking trips and canoe trips. I even enjoyed a survival camp week. The only out-camp that I missed was a bicycle camp. I never saw the need to go on a bicycle camp when I could stay home and ride my bike. I could never figure out why one would bring a bike to camp and call that camping. The older I got, the more I was in awe of the camp staff. They were the most wonderful people in the world.

"Above all the paid staff was a volunteer counselor who was a minister in NYC. He did difficult ministry in a dangerous urban setting. Each year he volunteered for a week to lead the backpacking trips. He brought a carload of inner-city kids with him from his church. These he registered for in-camp experiences while he led the high school campers out on the trail. He was a free spirit, the very kind of man that high school students gravitated to, but the man who gave parents nightmares.

"Dan was a political liberal who had burned his draft card, read avidly from Henry David Thoreau, and regularly participated in civil disobedience on the streets of New York. We talked politics and frequently about the Beatles. What was more important is that he introduced me to the politics of the Reformed Church and guided me into thinking of discernment. How does one know if you are called to ministry? This was an important question for me in high school, as I was contemplating this possibility in preparation for college.

"I thought the world of Dan and would have done anything for him. He had a charisma and a rebellious streak that I found attractive. He invited me to visit him at his church in New York. I wanted to but never found the time. Maybe it was laziness or perhaps it was God's providence.

"One of my life's dreams was fulfilled my senior year of high school, when I was accepted into the counselor in training program and successfully passed the training. I stayed on staff for the rest of the summer. As training counselors, we were not paid. We were given staff t-shirts and ten dollars' worth of credit each week at the camp store, and that was more compensation than we required. All of us would have paid to be on staff. Our group had grown up at this camp and dreamed of being part of the 'team.'

"That summer was the best summer of my life. I was at camp, which was my definition of heaven, and was now part of the staff that I had grown up idolizing. The little kids at camp all looked at me as being 'cool' in the same way as I had always looked at the staff. At the end of the summer I would be going out to Hope College. I carried my acceptance letter with me and read it over whenever I had a free moment. I was on top of the world.

"A new relationship began for me halfway through that summer. It was with the camp director, Reverend Harry Haskell. He had been the director of the camp as long as anyone could remember. He was my parents' age, with kids just slightly older than myself. There were three of them whom I had known as campers and now all three were on staff. To a camper, Harry was unapproachable. To staff, he was a big brother. He held to an 'open door' policy where staff could always stop by his house to talk.

"One evening, after our vespers, I asked him, 'How does a person know that he is called to ministry?' He told me to stop by the next evening to talk. I did. He offered me bourbon. I debated telling him that I was underage but chose to keep that bit of information to myself. We sat for two hours sipping whiskey and exploring ministerial discernment. It was a wonderful evening for me to be treated like an adult, and even shown such respect by a minister.

"When I look back at that night now I can't help but wonder why a minister would offer whiskey to such a young person at a Christian camp. At the time, it was wonderful and I appreciated it. I shudder now when I think of it. It was absolutely inappropriate.

"That summer also I had a chance to see Dan once again, as he came for his week of backpacking. I had the privilege of him dropping off two of his kids to my cabin that I was counseling for the week. I was flattered when he told me that he requested his kids to be in my cabin. It was one more sign that I had really arrived where I wanted to be.

"The summer ended too quickly, and I was off to college. Before I left my heaven, I had my interview with Reverend Harry. I was thrilled as he complimented my work, before handing me a contract to be a counselor the following summer. I quickly signed it, shook his hand, and left for home. In four days I would begin my career as a Hope College student.

"Life in college was an adventure, and at the end of my first year I came back to my 'paradise in the wood.' This time I came early, as staff members were required to do. We set up the camp and received more training. We greeted old friends and met several new ones. I walked a bit taller and with more confidence, now that I had a year of college behind me. I started what I thought would be the best summer of my life, even better than the one before.

"I got to see Dan again, and cared for his church kids for a week. I sipped whiskey with Harry and talked theology until late at night. By mid-August I was planning for my return to college and my next year on staff the following summer. Life was good and I never dreamed that things could crash so quickly. In one night, my heaven collapsed and an idol of mine fell."

I watched the room staring at Ralph. Most of all I looked at Will who sat next to Ralph and was hearing this story for the first time. Ralph no longer looked shamed or guilty. He showed no signs of depression. All of those emotions were now replaced by raw rage. His neck veins popped, and his fists were clenched.

He was breathing hard, and his breaths began to sound more like growls. Will instinctively moved a bit away from him. Those of us who had heard his story before were less upset by his anger.

"That bastard hurt his children, and I hope he burns in hell," Ralph concluded, his anger still palpable. Will moved his chair a foot away from Ralph and was now even closer to me. I set my hand on his shoulder to comfort and calm him.

"I was in the cabins that week, so I missed the staff meeting that the others had in the morning. After breakfast and cleanup we went down for swimming lessons. The whole staff looked as though the world had ended. My kids went into the water and I asked Ellen why everyone looked so down. 'You don't want to know,' was all she said. I looked to find Harry's kids, knowing that they would know what was going on. They were nowhere to be seen.

"Finally I grabbed Evette, an exchange counselor from Australia. I asked her why everyone was tense, and she gave me the same response as Ellen had. I pushed, insisting on knowing. Finally, she relented.

"'Reverend Harry started to molest John last night. John went to him to discuss some family problems he is having. He plied him with whiskey and started to molest him. John fought him off, ran, and got to a phone. Instead of calling home he called the police. They were here late last night and took Harry away in handcuffs.'

"I felt sick to my stomach and Evette realized it. Lovingly she pulled me away from the waterfront and into the woods. It was then that I began vomiting. John, that poor, troubled, counselor in training, was given whiskey and molested. How was I lucky enough to avoid the same fate?

"'That is sick,' I said, stating the obvious.

"'You haven't heard the worst. With the police here and feeling safe, his kids came forward and reported that he had been molesting them since they can remember.'

"My heart beat fast enough to make me fear a heart attack, and my vomiting continued. One of my idols was a child molester. My heaven sheltered the worst abuse of all: child abuse. A man who I had trusted and idolized had betrayed me.

"By evening vespers, it seemed that every minister in the country had assembled at camp. The entire board of directors had been gathered. They met with the staff and told us to listen carefully, and observe campers to see if there might be other victims. I half-listened to them, not hearing much, but basking in anger.

"I spent the final two weeks of the summer angry at Harry and angry at God. How could a God whose Son had condemned anyone who hurt a child have allowed this to happen? Why had God not struck him down with a heart attack before he could hurt a child?

"At my exit interview before I left, the assistant camp director handed me a contract for the following year. I told him that I didn't want to come back, as this year was too painful. He encouraged me to pray about it. I never did. That night I threw the contract in the garbage and vowed never to return. I spent my next year angry with Harry and angry with God. I lived in anger. My paradise was lost.

"I drove the memories of my paradise lost from my mind and continued my path to ministry. The camp ghosts caught up with me eight years later. I was a young minister in Hoboken when I saw a picture of my friend Dan on the news. A mob in his neighborhood was vowing to kill him. Three of the boys in his church came forward with a story of him molesting and raping them. The feeling of devastating betrayal came back to me.

"A month later Dan called me and asked me if I would write a letter to the NYC prosecutor, testifying that nothing in my interactions with him would lead me to believe that he could be a molester. I pushed him to make sure that he was innocent, and he assured me that he was. When I asked him why these kids would say such things, he told me that family members were molesting them and that he was a 'safer' target. His protests and civil disobedience against the NY power structure also had made him enemies among the prosecutors.

"Dan convinced me of his innocence and I wrote a letter of support for him. It was about a year later that I found out he had jumped bail, moved to the Netherlands, and was claiming that nothing in the Bible precluded man-boy love."

Again I watched and listened. Various group members moved to stabilize dishes that were vibrating toward the edge. Ralph's rage was still apparent, as he once again pulled unconscious memories into the conscious mind.

"I supported a child molester. That makes me guilty as well. When I heard of Dan's remarks from a clergy colleague I stopped at a liquor store on the way home and bought a bottle of vodka—the first I had purchased since my college days. At home I opened it and prepared to drink myself into oblivion. My wife called Jack, who arrived within an hour at my door. Jack put the bottle out of my sight and we began to talk about betrayal and being cast out of paradise. We talked a long time, but the nightmares still remain."

He stood and stared as if he were seeing something that he was not looking at. His flashbacks had returned. I moved to embrace him.

"Ralph, come back. Ralph, it's Jack. You're safe. Come back."

Laura moved in behind him and began massaging his scalp as she hummed in a low tone. It had no rhythm and no melody, it was simply a hum. Her hands were the hands of a healer. I had seen her work before. Healing was her gift.

"Ralph, come back. Christ and his people are here."

I could feel his body relax as I began to walk him toward the armchairs of the living room. Laura followed, not breaking her rhythm of hands or hum. As we left, Harvey rose and began clearing the table. Soon Laura and I sat with Ralph; Will stood looking frightened. The other three did the necessary but not glamorous work of cleaning. We were a team—a team of the wounded, but a team nevertheless.

13

Christ's Healing

Ralph had come back to real time and was composed by the time the kitchen had been cleaned and the dishes put away. Madeline and Harvey brought the communion ware, a small bowl of olive oil, and the talking stick, and placed these on the table. The group had circled up once again.

Ralph sat quietly on the small couch with his head in his hands with Laura sitting at his side. The eyes of the others were all on Will. They paid more attention to him than they had to the others. We had heard one another's stories over the years but only I had heard what Will had to share.

"Will," I said as I picked up the stick and handed it to him. "It is your turn. This is why we are here. It is time to tell your story."

Reluctantly he took the stick from me, rolled it in his hand, and scanned the circle of the six of us. Did he trust us? *Could* he trust us? He took a deep breath, looked once more into the eyes of the circle members, and decided to trust enough to begin.

His story was shorter than most and he told it quickly. There were times that I felt he was racing just to get it over with. I was worried about Ralph from his reaction and wondered how

Will would do with his first time describing his trauma to the group. I looked back and forth between these men, wondering if I would need to intervene.

The group sat quietly and attentively as Will began. He stammered and stuttered his way through the memories as he kept his eyes glued to the small table in the center of the circle. He appeared distraught but controlled. I doubted that he would have told his story if he had not heard the previous six stories. The healing power of this group, besides God's presence, was the knowledge it gave that none of these wounded disciples were alone.

Perhaps halfway, or maybe two-thirds of the way through Will's recounting, Ralph snapped to attention. He sat straight up quickly enough to alarm Laura, who moved away to grant him more space. Ralph attached his gaze on Will, and squinted in a pained sympathetic way. He was resonating with the story, connecting with Will on a spiritual level. These two had souls joined over the grief of hurt children. Ralph looked as though he was wishing to leap out of the chair but was restraining himself.

Finally, Will, the new initiate to our circle, finished his story and threw the stick onto the table before holding his head in his hands. As always happens, group members rise to hug and affirm those who have told a tale of hurt. Ralph was the first one up, and shot across the room to Will. I noticed the size difference between the two as he hugged the smaller man. Ralph, a towering six-foot-four, was holding Will who was barely five-foot-eight. Ralph had learned how to comfort people in the same way that I did. In a swift motion, he lifted Will from the chair and held him up in his arms.

"It's not your fault, Will. It's not your fault. You are guilty of nothing," he said.

Ralph, like most of us, was like George Bailey of *It's a Wonderful Life*. None of us are as good at self-care as we ought to be, but we rise to aid and protect others. George saved himself when he jumped to aid Clarence the angel. Ralph rose out of himself for the sake of Will.

The others had gathered around by now with their healing touches and affirmation. This wounded man was loved and comforted. Could he find the grace to accept forgiveness and begin to heal? That was up to God and him. Our circle could only be a catalyst for the grace of God.

For perhaps ten minutes I allowed the hugs and affirmation. There were few dry eyes. Will had found a group in which he was accepted and could heal. I decided that it was time to begin the next step of healing. I stood in my "preaching position" in the center of the room and used my best preaching voice to begin.

"Are any among you suffering?" I proclaimed, and the group ended the embracing and came back to the circle for the responses that they had grown used to from the *Reformed Church in America Healing Liturgy*, adapted from the book of James.

"They should pray," the group shouted out.

"Are any cheerful?" I continued.

"They should sing songs of praise." The response came back to me.

"Are any among you sick?"

"They should call for the elders of the church and have them pray over them, anointing them with oil in the name of the Lord," came the final group response.

"The prayer of faith will save the sick, and the Lord will raise them up; and anyone who has committed sins will be forgiven." I finished the words of our liturgy for healing.

Laura guided Will to his spot in the circle. We stood in the same positions we had when we sat around the table for our meal. Harvey, the first of the group, sat on my left, and Will the newest member on my right. It was time to bless each other with oil in the name of the Lord Jesus and seek the healing that only he could provide.

The group surrounded Harvey laying hands on him. Laura again guided Will and showed him how to participate in this ceremony of healing. He joined in placing his hand upon Harvey's shoulder. I picked up the bowl of oil, wet my thumb with it, and made the sign of the cross on Harvey's forehead.

"Harvey," I said, "May the hands of the Great Physician, Jesus Christ, rest upon you now in divine blessing and healing. May the cleansing stream of his pure life fill your whole being, body, mind, and spirit, to strengthen and heal you. Amen."

It was almost deafening as the other six repeated the "Amen."

We held Harvey for a moment before moving toward Laura and the group surrounded her with our love. The others laid hands on her shoulders as I refreshed the oil on my thumb and made the sign on her head. I made the invocation again and once more the group responded.

I continued around the circle as we blessed each member. At last we came to Will, who looked overwhelmed. Perhaps he had never seen the healing service celebrated. Many members haven't seen this forty-year-old liturgy of our church; it is one of our best-kept secrets. Perhaps the emotions of the room were too much for him. Maybe it was the Holy Spirit working on him. No matter what the reason, Will looked to be at the breaking point.

The other five placed their hands on him, and for the final time I placed a thumb on a forehead. I could feel his head tremble as I made the sign of the cross and repeated the prayer of blessing. I thought he would collapse as his knees weakened with emotion. Laura, the mother and healer, and Ralph, who had bonded with him over children, held him firmly. Like a mother and father comforting a child these two held with gentle firmness. We waited as he cried his weakness out and his strength returned.

Finally, it was my turn. My sisters and brothers gathered to bless me in the same way that I sought to bless them. I felt their warmth. I felt their support. I felt the Holy Spirit. I felt the peace that only Christ can give.

It was a few minutes before the group began to disburse from me and back into the wider circle. Our relationship with one another was wonderful, nurturing and healing. More important was our relationship with Jesus. It was only he who could heal. And so the last part of our circle meeting began. It was communion with one another, but most importantly with Jesus the Christ. The chalice and the bread were ready. We only had to begin.

How does one minister lead communion for other ministers? It is not easy. It is like one chef cooking for a group of cooks, or a musician performing for a group of professional instrumentalists. In performing such functions, I need to remind myself that I am doing nothing; it is the Spirit that is doing it all. God could get a trail rock to do this if He so desired. For some reason I was chosen, and I pray that God uses me. As a wire conducts electricity to a light bulb, so I must somehow conduct God's grace to his wounded.

I picked up the copies of our Eucharist liturgy from the table and passed them around. We all knew this liturgy well and most of us conducted it on a monthly basis. It was always different receiving it as opposed to delivering it. My communion Sundays were filled mostly with leading worship for various congregations. Every now and then I had the honor of attending a church service during communion and it was a rare pleasure to sit and be served. The six before me now readied themselves for the privilege. I began our communion prayer:

"The Lord be with you."

"And also with you," the group replied.

"Lift up your hearts!"

"We lift them up to the Lord," the reply came back.

I continued with our liturgy. "Holy and right it is, and our joyful duty to give thanks to you at all times and in all places, O Lord our Creator, almighty and everlasting God. You created heaven with all its hosts and the earth with all its plenty. You have given us life and being, and preserve us by your providence. But you have shown us the fullness of your love in sending into the world your Son, Jesus Christ, the eternal Word, made flesh for us and for our salvation.

"For the precious gift of this mighty Savior who has reconciled us to you we praise and bless you, O God. With your whole Church on earth and with all the company of heaven we worship and adore your glorious name."

"Holy, holy, holy Lord, God of power and might, heaven and earth are full of your glory. Hosanna in the highest! Blessed is he who comes in the name of the Lord. Hosanna in the highest!" they responded.

I waited for a moment, as was the custom of our liturgy.

"Most righteous God, we remember in this Supper the perfect sacrifice offered once on the cross by our Lord Jesus Christ for the sin of the whole world. In the joy of his resurrection and in expectation of his coming again, we offer ourselves to you as holy and living sacrifices. Together we proclaim the mystery of the faith."

It did not take long for the response to be returned to me by the group.

"Christ has died! Christ is risen! Christ will come again!"

I now completed the communion prayer: "Send your Holy Spirit upon us, we pray, that the bread which we break and the cup which we bless may be to us the communion of the body and blood of Christ. Grant that, being joined together in him, we may attain to the unity of the faith and grow up in all things into Christ our Lord.

"And as this grain has been gathered from many fields into one loaf, and these grapes from many hills into one cup, grant, O Lord, that your whole Church may soon be gathered from the ends of the earth into your kingdom. Even so, come, Lord Jesus!"

I picked up the round loaf of bread from the china plate on the table and broke it in half and said the words of institution:

"The Lord Jesus, the same night he was betrayed, took bread and when he had given thanks, he broke it and gave it to them, saying, 'Take, eat; this is my body which is given for you: do this in remembrance of me.'"

I broke the loaf in half and passed one half to my left and the other to my right. Each person, in turn, ripped a piece from it and held it while I continued.

"After the same manner also, he took the cup when they had supped, saying 'this cup is the new testament in my blood; this do, as often as you drink it, in remembrance of me.'"

I passed the cup to my left. One at a time each group member dipped the bread into the cup and held it. At last the cup returned to me and I ripped a piece of bread and dipped it into the cup. I held it up.

"The bread which we break is the communion of the body of Christ and the cup of blessing that we bless is the communion of the blood of Christ."

In one movement, we each partook of the bread and the wine. We were silent as we let God's Spirit come over us and into us, speaking to us, comforting us, and healing us.

At last we moved closer to one another, linking arms on shoulders as if we were in a football huddle. We circled the table with the talking stick, the oil for healing, and our communion elements. I began our final prayer.

"We thank you great God for this communion shared with you, one another, and with all the saints of your church. We thank you for these your servants who have been wounded in service to you and those you have given them to care for.

"Heal them, we pray, by your precious blood, that these wounds might no longer give pain and that they will be empowered for future work among the people that you have given them to nourish.

"As you healed so many while you walked the earth, heal these your servants for your service.

"We pray in Jesus' name. Amen."

"Amen!" was the loud refrain from the group, but we did not part from our huddle with the closing of the prayer. Our circle continued as we felt the warmth and spirit of one another. We cried together, and held onto our colleagues in ministry.

14

Welcome Home

How long did we hold onto one another? I don't know. We did not wish to leave the huddle. We could feel the warmth of one another, the Spirit, and the healing of touch. Gradually I could feel Will's strength returning. His legs were firm again and now supporting his weight. He no longer looked like a man who didn't wish to live. He no longer leaned on my shoulders.

We were quiet for the first time all day, and I could hear the breathing of all in the circle. I remembered being taught in seminary that the Hebrew word for "spirit" was the same word as "wind." Literally the Spirit of God is the Wind of God. When God breathed air into Adam's nostrils and he became a living man, it was Wind that God was breathing. Now I heard the living wind of God flowing in and out of God's healing servants.

A banging on the door, the hinges creaking, and the deep voice of Dean echoing through the room interrupted the quiet circle.

"Jack," Dean bellowed, "I have another group coming in an hour. I need you to start getting cleaned up." He had come in like a whirlwind, in contrast to the quiet breathing of our group.

He stopped with embarrassment as he saw us standing quietly in a circle. Perhaps he thought we were praying. We broke our huddle and turned toward him.

"Dean," I said, "We will be out within the hour."

"Thank you," he said, still looking a bit embarrassed. We were not surprised when he added, "Please make sure it is clean enough for the next group. I don't have as much prep time as I usually have."

"We will have it ready. Where are your cleaning supplies?"

"This way," he said. I turned to follow when Will and Ralph stopped me.

"We have this, Jack," said Will, now fully engaged. He looked like a minister of Christ again. The two followed Dean to fetch vacuums as Laura and Walter began cleaning up the communion ware. The others began the kitchen cleanup. I stood in the center of the room and wondered if I had a purpose. Soon I was watching the others scurry around and heard the two vacuums, as Will and Ralph began the floors under Dean's direction.

Who cleaned up after the Last Supper? Does anyone know? We are told the disciples followed Jesus out to the garden of Gethsemane. Were there only the twelve? Did more disciples follow? Did any of the women who accompanied Jesus and fund his ministry follow as well? Did they stay and clean up? Did the owner of the building where the dinner was held have servants to do the dirty work?

And what about when Jesus met the disciples on the road to Emmaus? Where did Jesus get the bread from before he broke it? Who cleaned up after he disappeared, and the two disciples ran back to Jerusalem? Did Jesus leave messes behind him?

We in the circle do not quite have the privileges that Jesus had. We had to clean after our meetings. This group had bonded and worked as a team to make the room spotless. Soon Laura was asking for my car keys to load the trunk. Ultimately we finished the job in thirty minutes instead of an hour. Dean seemed pleased as he inspected. We gathered outside for our final ritual, the circle of blessing.

With the car packed and the building clean we gathered in a circle in the parking lot. We stood as we always do, in the order of when we each joined the group. Once again, Harvey was on my left and Will on my right. I began our final ritual. I left the outside of the circle and stood in front of Harvey.

"Harvey," I said, "Be healed and be blessed in the name of the Father, Son, and Holy Spirit."

I moved to my right and stopped in front of Laura and repeated the blessing. Next I stopped at Walter, and then to Madeline, before I finished with Ralph and Will. When I had completed the circle, Harvey began the same route, echoing my words. Each person walked the ring and blessed each member of the group. There were hugs and there were tears.

"Ladies and gentlemen, our circle meeting is completed," I said. "Today we are the Circle of Seven. Whenever someone needs us you will be summoned and we will gather again. We will help heal others, even as we are healing. We are one and we are bonded forever."

There were hugs all around before we climbed into our cars and headed back home. The cars of the next group to use Calvin House passed us on the road. They would be beginning their encounters in this holy place, even as our time there had ended. Laura sat quietly meditating in the back seat. Before we arrived at the main road Will was in a sound sleep in the front seat. I drove trying to cope with the disquieting silence of my companions.

It was dusk as we drove up the long driveway to Laura's home. Will woke and Laura kissed us each goodbye before scampering up the path into her house. I waited until the door opened. Her Rottweilers welcomed her and she greeted them with kisses. She let them out so they could run and gain relief. I turned the car around and headed down the driveway.

Will returned to sleep as we drove toward his home. Within forty minutes we were there. For the second time, I pulled into his driveway and turned to him.

"Will, you do know that if you kill yourself you will be hurting your family and the other six members in this group, don't you?"

"Yes, Jack. I understand. I see things better now."

"No longer depressed and suicidal?"

"I was never really suicidal, just depressed."

"That's debatable," I said, smiling. "You will hurt people if you hurt yourself. Do you understand this?"

"Yes, Jack, I understand."

"Good. That is what I hoped to hear. I'll call you in a few days. Be nice to your wife and kids. They worry about you."

"I will, Jack. Thank you."

"You're welcome."

He left the car and began walking toward the house. I waited until the door opened. Ginny embraced as she waved to me. I drove off, anxious to be home with my wife.

On the way home I prayed, "Thank you, God; thank you, thank you."